LESSONS OF
FAIRSIZED
CREEK

LESSONS OF FAIRSIZED CREEK

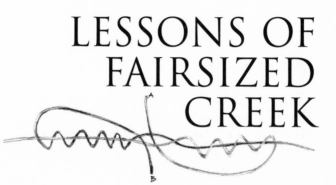

12 WAYS TO CATCH MORE TROUT ON THE FLY

JOHN HUBER

ILLUSTRATED BY DAYNA SMITH

PRUETT
PUBLISHING
BOULDER
2002

Printed in the United States of America

11 10 09 08 07 06 05 04 03 02   5 4 3 2 1

Library of Congress Cataloging-in-Publication Data

Huber, John, 1967–
     Lessons of fairsized creek : 12 ways to catch more trout on the fly /
     John Huber ; illustrated by Dayna Smith.
          p.   cm.
     ISBN 0-87108-917-3 (alk. paper)
     I. Title.

PS3608.U54 L47 2001
813'.54—dc21   2001031861

Cover and book design by Paulette Livers Lambert
Book composition by Lyn Chaffee

For my Grandmother Elvira Huber, who is the root and strength of my family tree, and for the six newest leaves, Rachael, Logan, Nathan, Elizabeth, Carly, and Natalie. May you all discover the richness, peace, and magic of our natural world.

CONTENTS

PREFACE

E very so often people will hear, taste, or smell something that will trigger a sharp childhood memory, and sometimes people find an activity that links them directly back to those preteen years when all was right with the world. They have found out that there is a way to play, just like they did when they were kids.

Fly fishing. What other activity allows us to meander hip-deep up rivers or jump small meadow streams, collect things like flies and boxes, call friends to come play with us, and sit or nap under shady trees with the sound of running water ever present? Sometimes when fly fishing we camp or hike or even float in inner tubes. We chase bugs and collect live specimens, we hoard our favorite toys, and we often refuse to share secrets. Sometimes, though, we blab secrets as quickly as we hear them.

Does this description sound a bit like a seven-year-old? Fly fishing is synonymous with recess or even the almighty summer vacation. The upside to all of this is people can find a doorway to their past and revel in the sheer joy of just playing for the sake of playing. The downside to all of this—well, there is no downside.

Fly fishing has become an easy-to-access pastime that is widely accepted. It is regarded as a very sensible use of one's time. It is pleasing to the eye, the soul, and often the ego. A sport that at one time was intimidating to break into is now made easily accessible to those looking for a lifetime activity. The result of this new age in fly angling has been an increase in the number of anglers on our nation's blue-ribbon streams.

Ask any full-time guide in the profession, and he or she will tell you story after story of running into more people every year.

Streams that once were the private playground of a few adventurous individuals have now become destinations that people from all over the world look forward to playing in themselves. The result of this increase in angler numbers has in turn increased the degree of difficulty when it comes to the ultimate goal, catching fish.

The following is a story about friends and fishing. The purpose is not so much to tell a story as it is to prime a fly angler for today's tougher conditions and educated fish. Each chapter presents a technique or idea that today's angler can use to increase his or her catch rate on all waters and definitely those that see a fair amount of angler numbers.

The book represents twelve chapters of technique. Some are new and some are old. Ultimately, the fish decide whether any technique is good or bad. Raising angler awareness regarding technique is the goal of this book, but the underlying tone that I hope the angler takes away is one of kindness. Sure, our streams are more crowded, but can anyone really blame someone for wanting to pursue something that is so fun? Rest assured, none of us were here first; someone has always been on the water before us, and plenty will come after. Should fly anglers as a group press for more special regulations? Yes. In the meantime, should we deal with it, smile, and be kind to one another? Yes.

Catching fish is merely the by-product of going fishing. It is the act of fishing itself that ultimately is the goal. All anglers know this, but not everyone is aware that they know it. If catching a fish or fishing a "spot" is going to ruin someone's good time, then it's time to ask why you're fishing. The flip side is if someone is ruining your good time. Well, an angler with skills is a versatile angler that doesn't need much beyond the rod, the vest, and some water. It is hard to upset an angler that can catch fish anywhere, under any conditions. I hope this book takes you, the reader, one step closer to this next level.

Best of luck on the water, and please say hello should we ever meet on the stream.

ACKNOWLEDGMENTS

This is where I get to say thank you to all the people that help make my odd world go around. Of course the first person I wish to thank is Jim Pruett who gave me a chance to write this book. Jim is the rare soul who can manage to put trust in the obsessive behaviors of the full-time angler. I started writing this book about a year ago and have had three addresses and telephone numbers in this short time up to now, but Jim never flinched. He has obviously seen this fish-chasing behavior before and has learned to tap this impulsive energy for better or worse.

Thank you also to Dayna Smith, who did the drawings for this book. She has the kind of talent I'm jealous of. Her skill is obvious, and I'm sure we will see more of her work in the future.

Thanks to my parents Chuck and Connie who have supported my obsessive behavior as well. A whole lot of school got paid for before I went on this permanent fishing trip and I am lovingly grateful to them for giving me the peace to take it. School is where I learned the value of enjoying my life and learned the philosophy of fulfillment. I would do it all again for the knowledge I gained.

Thanks to the rest of my family: my grandmother Elvira Huber; my aunts Mary, Jean Ann, and Barbara Huber; and my uncles Francis Huber and David Haner; as well as my sisters Cathy Nickerson, Laura Veasy, and Jane Nelson and their beautiful families. I suppose if the life of a permanent angler is akin to walking a thin line, then they are my net. I hope I can be as equally supportive to them.

I want to thank Terry Ring, Dave Faltings, Jim Holcomb, Jerry Eder, Brett Drummond, Richie Thurston, and Mark Osmer at Silver Creek Outfitters, in Ketchum, Idaho, for making guiding fun again.

Many thanks go out to Bill and Marnee Wirth, Mike and Laura Shannon, Bruce and Ann Blume, Doug and Debbie Shepherd, John and Nancy Shepherd, Gary and Missy Lipton, and David and Pat Sias, who have all been my friends and supporters over many years of throwing fly lines together. May we throw many, many more.

A special thanks to David and Edyth Goodman and their families, who have helped me with my saltwater affliction, as well as a big thanks for being friends and mentors on days when the water has been a little rough.

I have three friends in Colorado to thank, Jeff Schizas, Mike Manos, and Stuva Maniatis, who remind me several times a year, how much I enjoy fishing with friends. They make me aware to cherish the fleeting moments we have with those who don't live up or down the valley from us. You guys are welcome to wet a line with me anytime.

I lied, I have four fishing friends in Colorado. Thanks for the loaner again Eric Lyon. Call me and we'll go fishing sometime.

I also want to thank Ale Berckmans Mitchell for the guidance and encouragement she has given me. Also, a big thanks to Jim Cole for never taking his line out of the water.

Finally, thanks to my daily fishing partners, Mike Witthar, Mike Bordenkircher, Jonathan Wagoner, Brett Williams, and

Greg Thomas. I cannot say enough about these guys. They are pretty much willing to go anywhere, just about anytime, in the pursuit of fish and fun, and they're all good at both. Some days we find them, some days we don't, but I never enjoy fishing more than when I'm doing it with these guys.

INTRODUCTION

FAIRSIZED CREEK

On a particular run, in a particular river, sits a rainbow trout. Let's name him Terrance the Trout. Terrance is a big buck, with a bright red stripe and big mature spots on his back and sides. He is a very respectable twenty-inch rainbow.

He is swimming, or shall I say hovering, in very shallow, pyramid-shaped riffles adjacent to a deep back eddy in a long run. The run starts as white water and eventually calms enough to form the riffles, which in turn calm and become a long flat glide. The left side of the run is deep and overhung by denser willows and rock cliffs. The right side of the run is a gently sloping gravel bar that runs to a dense stand of cottonwood trees.

Let's call the river Fairsized Creek, which is a tributary of Long-Known River. Fairsized Creek was at one time a quiet fishery used by local anglers, but in the last few years it has seen as many angler days as the popular bigger brother that it feeds. Terrance was a fry back in these quieter times, but he has grown up in an age of increased anglers. He has been caught and released several times through the course of his life, but each day, each year, he seemingly grows a little wiser as well as bigger. Today he is intent on eating every trico spinner he sees

coming down his small feeding lane in the riffle near the head of the run he occupies.

Terrance isn't going to move from side to side more than a half an inch to ingest insects, because Terrance has been fished over roughly five days a week during this particular summer. He has been fooled, hooked, and landed a few times already this season, but Terrance was desperate to eat in the early months of summer. Now insects are plentiful, and Terrance gets to pick and choose what he will eat and he will do so when he wants to.

The hatches and spinner falls are pretty much one after another on the creek, as summer's light and cool mountain waters meet for three or four, always too short, summer months in the Rockies. Also seen in greater numbers during these months are anglers who are hoping to catch the best of summer's hatches as well as the trout that subsequently feed on them. After three years in this creek, Terrance is no stranger to the hazards of eating insects.

Before the days of proactive catch and release, the problem of the educated trout didn't often come into play. Today, the word *educated* is often used to describe a fish in any particular fishery that has adjusted to his environment in order not to get caught. This means that the fish has adopted certain habits or traits that produce fewer horrifying moments while it is dining.

So here, on this bright August morning, Terrance the educated trout sips trico spinners greedily, despite the fear of the hook. The word *hook* is used as if Terrance has a vocabulary. Actually, to Terrance, the moment we call hooking up is a moment in which a very angry insect (food to Terrance) begins stinging and hauling him around his aquatic world, despite his every attempt to let this insect go. The times he isn't able to expel the insect from his mouth, despite his struggles, the insect pulls him to a giant predator who then (in these well-regulated waters) always seemingly makes the mistake of letting Terrance regain his strength and make a break for it.

Terrance knows that this can happen on any given mouthful, but Terrance also knows that the less he strays from his favorite feeding lane, the less the angry insect shows up. Terrance doesn't really understand this in the true sense as much as his instinct tells him one act is better for him than another. Hence, by the time this August morn has dawned, Terrance has become educated to the extreme.

The first one to see Terrance this morning is Bobby. Bobby has been fly fishing for a few years and has a good handle on the basics. He can cast well, knows his knots, and has a basic understanding of aquatic insects. He has gotten to the water early this morning in an attempt to hike up the river a bit, before the morning rise starts, but it is already well under way when he arrives.

CHAPTER 1

A HATCH IS A HATCH, AND A SPINNER FALL IS A SPINNER FALL

In Bobby's mind, the hatch is on. He had hiked upstream, and fish are sipping flies one after another all the way up and down the run. Besides the bugs that cover the water, he can also see millions of insects in the air. They are apparently all flying upstream in an orderly fashion. Bobby grabs his telescoping bug net from an inner vest pocket and swings it through the air. Upon examining the net's contents, he decides the bug he is looking at is the infamous size 22 Trico that the clerk at the local fly shop had told him about. The clerk also told him how great of a rise this insect brings on, and now Bobby can hardly contain his excitement.

"This hatch is amazing! What a morning this is going to be," he says to himself as he wades into the cool stream. He scans the water for eager fish. After surveying the run for a minute or so, he notices a particularly large nose poking out of the riffles on the far side of the creek. He wades carefully and positions himself for an easy twenty-five-foot cast. Bobby breathes deeply and imagines the crisp mountain air cleaning his lungs. He begins to peel line from his reel.

Bobby is both correct and wrong. The trico is in fact the insect that has the water boiling with trout on this particular day. His mistake is common: It isn't the hatch that is on. What's happening is indeed the trico, but as is most common in regard to angling during an event of this insect, the spinner fall is in full swing. The hatch had already happened in the dawn and predawn hours of this same morning.

Bobby takes his favorite dry fly out of a box labeled SMALL DRIES. It is a brilliantly tied size 22 Adams, which would have been a perfectly acceptable fly to fish had Bobby been on the water at 5:30 this morning during the major hatch of tricos. It is now 8:30 and already getting hot. The insects that the fish are eating have already spun and are dead. Bobby ties a twelve-foot leader and attaches another eighteen inches of 6X tippet to it. He ties the fly on, dresses it with floatant, and is ready to go. Bobby watches the big rainbow rise three more times and then begins to false cast. His presentation is perfect, and he lays the fly down beautifully, exactly two feet upstream from the big fish's nose.

TERRANCE EATS, eats again, eats once more, and then suddenly notices a lone dun coming into his lane, which is filled with spent winged tricos.

At around 7:00 A.M., as the spinner fall began to happen, Terrance was indeed seeing both late-hatching duns and early falling spinners, but for the last hour, he had only seen spent winged insects enter his lane.

A few hours earlier, the late-hatching duns were on the water, yet were quick to lift off as the air temperature was rising quickly. Due to the particularly warm air this morning, the duns were very active as soon as the sun crested the horizon. They were lively, with an upright wing, which they fluttered in an attempt to dry them. They would lift off the water in short bursts until their wings were rigid enough and they could finally fly to the nearest streamside vegetation.

The spinners on the water now are mostly dead or in the throes of death. Many have changed color, turning a dull brown. The majority of tricos are completely dead or spent, lying with their wings flat on the surface film.

To Terrance, the spent winged spinners are a delight. He can feed freely without worrying about the insect flying off at the last minute, therefore expending as little energy as possible. There are times when Terrance prefers the dun, but this is often on cooler mornings when duns have more trouble lifting off the water and are easier targets. This is especially true during the early fall season.

For now, Terrance dines away in peace, until suddenly, after an hour of steadily feeding on nothing but spinners, here comes what appears to be an upright winged dun. Well, luckily for Terrance, and unfortunately for Bobby, Terrance ate a stray dun like this two days ago, and that was a very angry insect. Since that time, Terrance's instincts tell him to only eat the down-winged insect. He drops slightly deeper into the river and waits.

Bobby watches, slightly surprised as his first cast of the season unfolds and delivers his fly on the dime. It seems to take an eternity for the fly to drift the two feet to the big trout's nose. Suddenly there is a bulge in the water, yet Bobby sees his fly all the way. It rides gently over the bulge in the water and on down the river. Bobby lifts the fly, false casts a second time, and then suddenly realizes there is no more target to cast to.

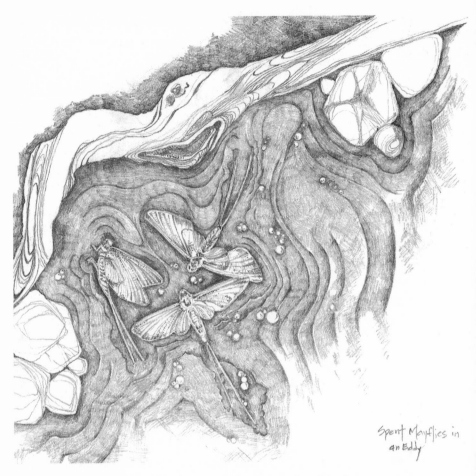

Spent Mayflies in
an Eddy

"You put him down with one cast," Bobby hears someone shout behind him.

Sure enough, on a log, near where the woods begin, sits a man. The man is large but is grinning, a gentle-giant sort. He has graying hair and a kind face. He stares back at Bobby, saying nothing else for the moment. Sometimes waders make a person look bigger than they really are, but in this case Bobby is pretty sure this man's appearance is no trick of the eye. The man is unshaven, and long silver hair lies across his shoulders. The man rises and walks over to Bobby, who begins fumbling for something to say.

As the man gets closer, Bobby finally responds, "I suppose he was leader shy, but I'll drop to 7X and wait for him to come back; I'm in no rush."

"You're in a rush to decorate that fish if you begin to use that 7X, mister," the stranger replies.

Bobby is stunned by this comment and says, "Well, Mister . . . ," but the stranger interrupts him.

"You can call me Jerry."

Bobby is perplexed but figures he can get back to fishing with a quick bit of sarcasm. "Well, Jerry, what do you suggest I do while the trout that you probably educated forgets that I'm here?"

Bobby thinks this snide remark will end this streamside conversation, but the large man only looks him over with a smile. He asks Bobby's name and explains that he meant no offense by his comment. As it turns out, Jerry lives just down the road on a small farm and is a local fishing guide. He explains to Bobby that he has never seen his car parked at the access and, like everyone he meets on the river, he just came over to say hello. He happened to arrive just as Bobby was slipping into the water, so he thought he would watch rather than break the young man's concentration.

Bobby is a bit embarrassed about his attitude and decides to relax a bit. "I'm sorry I barked at you, Jerry. I guess I was overly excited about that fish. I live in Big City, and I'm not used to total strangers being friendly." Bobby looks back to the water to see if the fish has renewed its feeding. "So, you're a local, Jerry; what do you do out here when you're not guiding?"

Jerry smiles and looks at the river. "I'm just a fishing guide, I suppose."

"You suppose?" Bobby asks.

"Well, sometimes it seems very surreal to me that I can do this for a living, in an odd sort of way. But never mind that, I've got the morning off." Jerry puts on his sunglasses and unzips his fleece collar.

Bobby nods and says, "Jerry, I know it's your day off and everything, but before you go, could you at least tell me what I did wrong with that fish?"

"Do you like roast beef?" Jerry asks.

The two of them sit on the bank and share a roast beef sandwich at about 9:00 A.M. They chat about Bobby's home in Big City and about Jerry's two bloodhounds, Skeets and Milo, whom they can hear barking in the back of Jerry's truck a quarter mile downriver.

Jerry finishes his roast beef and wipes his hands down the front of his waders. "Bobby, that fish over there is going to come back up, but before he does I want you to understand that a hatch is a hatch and a spinner fall is a spinner fall. Ten years ago I used to show these fish a size 16 Royal Wulff during the spinner fall, and they would eat it about half the time. Those days are gone, but I can't say enough about how much I've learned from these trout. Especially that one you were just throwing at. That guy has been living in this eddy for at least three years. He seems twice as educated as any fish in this run."

Jerry pauses and ponders for a second, then asks Bobby, "Do you have any down-winged fly patterns?"

Bobby looks at Jerry and is obviously confused. Jerry grabs a stone from the river and explains the life cycle of the typical river-born insect. "To put it as simply as I can, the insects that the fish are eating this morning are aquatic born, as you surely know. They hatched in the predawn hours this morning and are spinning now. You simply have to recognize the difference between the look of the dead insect versus the look of the live one. These fish, especially that big one, have seen enough imitations of real insects to know better than to eat anything but what they are keying on. In the case of this spinner fall and most others, there comes a point when the trout is going to focus on the down-winged insect simply because it is easier pickings. That is why I asked if you had another pattern to approach this morning's rise with."

As Jerry continued his explanation of bugs at a more individual level, Bobby searched through his fly boxes.

Fifteen minutes later, after this brief entomology lesson, Bobby sits and shakes his head and wonders why the last three guides he hired hadn't told him any of this. He recalls hearing a lot about casting and the merits of certain rod companies over the others, but he was told nothing about eggs, pupa, nymphs called clingers, and nest builders, or about duns, spinners, molting, and how this cycle is renewed every season by many different kinds of bugs. Jerry goes on to talk about the similar patterns of terrestrials like grasshoppers and cicadas and the importance of bait fish and leeches. Just about the time Bobby is overwhelmed with information, the two of them eyeball the river and, like a practiced duet, announce, "There he is!"

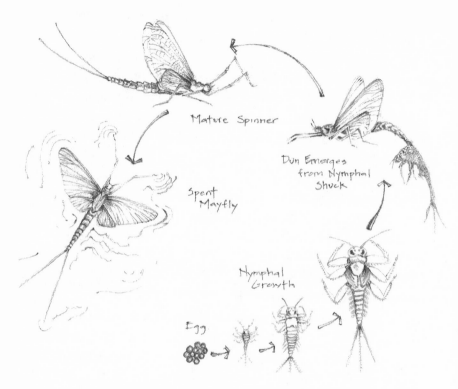

Mature Spinner

Dun Emerges
from Nymphal
Shuck

Spent
Mayfly

Nymphal
Growth

Egg

The big rainbow is not afraid anymore and is rising to the mats of dead tricos that are now coming down the run. Bobby is again poised and ready to cast at the trout with a new Zing Wing, spent trico pattern Jerry has given him. Jerry sits on his log and gets ready to give Bobby a friendly I-told-you-so as soon as Bobby hooks into Terrance. What none of the three of them sees is the flock of twenty Mergansers, the dreaded fish-eating duck, which is about to land right smack in the middle of the run.

The ducks hit the water with a great commotion. Sure enough, every fish is down in seconds, and knowing the spinner fall won't last much longer, Bobby and Jerry quickly head upstream to the next run. Bobby hooks up consistently for the next forty-five minutes on the down-winged fly pattern, but he hooks nothing approaching the size of the monster he had first cast at this morning. He is not terribly upset, though. He caught a lot of nice fish and made a new friend in the process. The spinner fall finally begins to peter out.

"Hey, Bobby!" Jerry yells over the sound of water rushing around his legs. "Same place tomorrow? I'll meet you at the Donut Emporium at 6:00 A.M. sharp."

"I'll be there!" Bobby yells back as he releases a nice fourteen-inch cuttbow.

CHAPTER 2

KNOTS AND SHORTCUTS

A brilliant new day dawns in the Rocky Mountains. The air is crisp, preventing the two anglers from rolling their sleeves up and the windows of the truck down as they drive to the river together. They both tote hot cups of coffee, which they sip vigorously.

"I want another shot at that fish those birds scared yesterday," Bobby says as he stares out the window with a look of impending victory in his eyes. He is feeling the same enthusiasm he had experienced the day before. Jerry pulls his old truck into the access and sets a useless emergency brake. He is well aware that the brake doesn't work, but he likes the sound it makes. Fortunately, Fairsized Creek Valley is relatively flat. They both hop out of the cab and grab their gear from the truck's bed. Jerry's hounds howl with disapproval, and both anglers laugh at this display and head for the stream.

"I want you to catch that fish, too; I wouldn't have it any other way," Jerry says with a grin.

TERRANCE IS enjoying the quiet of the river this morning, but he remains on guard for any noise, shadow, or vibration that will alert him to potential trouble. The more he eats, though, the less alert he remains. There hasn't been the slightest disturbance in or above the water, and the food is becoming more and more abundant. Terrance starts to feed without ever really submerging. He becomes gluttonous, and bugs slip out of his gills as he eats faster than he can ingest.

JERRY SEES Terrance first, and he urges Bobby to wait and watch in order to get a sense of any feeding pattern. He is also quick to point out that even though this morning is slightly cooler than yesterday, you still can't see the insects that the fish are dining on. Apparently, it is going to be strictly spinners again this morning.

Jerry takes off his ball cap and swings it through the air. "Tricos are so easy to catch," he says as he looks adoringly at the tricos escaping from his hat.

Bobby proceeds to the water's edge and gives the top of his telescoping bug net a brief tap out of sight into its special Velcro pocket. Jerry puts his cap back on and has a seat on his favorite log so he can watch his new friend stalk the big trout that eluded him yesterday.

After watching the rise form a few more minutes, Bobby peels line from his reel and starts false casting to the big rainbow. Bobby is quite a good caster, and despite a small downstream breeze, he is able to lay his spinner pattern slightly upstream of the fish's nose with very little sound and no splash at all. He can't see his fly very well but knows it is in the area. He watches carefully for a pronounced rise form but sees nothing except the trout greedily smacking on dozens of dead bugs. Bobby casts again and is able to see his fly this time. It is close to the fish's nose, but the fly slides by, about two inches to the left of the fish. He casts again, and then again, but the fly just isn't landing quite where he needs it. On his fifth cast Bobby's fly lands two feet upstream of Terrance, and it is only half an inch off Terrance's nose when Terrance suddenly feels Bobby's tippet slide over his back.

There is a quick burst of water and Bobby sets the hook, but no one is home. In an instant, the big 'bow had gone to the depths of the back eddy, panicked by the feel of the line on his body. Bobby turns and wades back to the bank. He looks toward Jerry, and with his eyes lowered he simply says, "I guess I should have let you catch him."

"Hey, no worries, Bobby," Jerry says in an upbeat tone of voice. "That fish has been here for three years, and I know he'll be back tomorrow or even later this evening."

The two of them fish their way downriver for the next few hours, eventually stopping for a roast beef sandwich. This time Jerry has also toted along two lukewarm beers. They sit on the riverbank in the shade of a big cottonwood and talk about the morning's fishing.

"So what did I do wrong with that fish today, Jerry?" Bobby asks with a sigh and takes a swig from his beer.

Jerry thinks he knows what happened with the big 'bow in the morning but is waiting for Bobby to ask. "I think your issue is with the way you tied your leader and tippets, Bobby. May I see your leader set-up?"

Bobby unseats his fly and hands it to Jerry as he pulls some slack from the reel.

"I want to see your leader and tippet because I'm not sure you were truly covering the fish's rise," Jerry says. "You may have been off by an inch or two. I know that will catch most fish in this river, but that boy knows not to stray off his lane, and when you set the hook on him today, you were merely reacting to your line or something spooking him, although for a second it may have appeared that he was eating."

Jerry looks over the leader and, just as he suspected, he finds three surgeon's knots forming Bobby's leader.

"I can see that you cast very well, Bobby. I think the problem here is an issue with knots. It's not uncommon for beginning anglers to start the easy way, often favoring the easy-to-tie surgeon's knot over a hard-to-learn but easy-to-tie blood knot. It usually becomes a habit that few anglers change, even as their skill level increases in all other areas. I've heard countless anglers blame their eyesight and say that it keeps them from tying blood knots, but you have to see the same size line to tie a surgeon's knot. Knots are simple motor-skill memory in your fingers. Practice is a necessity, but a blood knot tied during commercial breaks while watching television, or during idle time on your front porch, is learned much easier than trying to tie one while fish are gulping at your feet. The fact is, if you can tie one, you can tie the other if you're willing."

Bobby cuts his friend off suddenly, "Jerry, I really think the breaking strength of the surgeon's knot is about the same as a blood knot; it can't make that much difference."

"It's not a breaking-strength issue," Jerry is quick to answer back. "Your problem is a hinge that is created by a surgeon's knot when the knot is tightened.

"If you look at my knot system, it is what I would call a straight-line knot. When I cast my line and lay my leader out

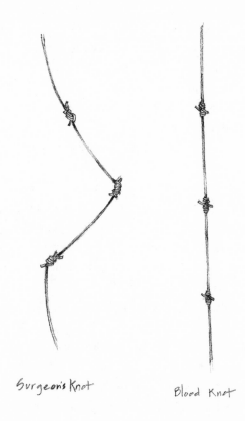

Surgeon's Knot   Blood Knot

straight, my fly is landing where I intend it to, whether or not I can see it. This becomes more and more important as small flies become less and less visible. You were casting to the right spot, but your leader was not doing what your mind told you it should have been doing. The three knots you have here hinge your line several inches left or right of what should be the true center, if your leader were to land perfectly straight. So when you can't see the fly, the initial placement on the presentation is of major importance in order to gauge if a fish is taking your artificial offering. Also keep in mind that the thicker the tippet diameter, the more pronounced the hinge becomes. This hinge effect may also be influenced by the water temperature as well, being that colder water is going to make the monofilament more rigid and more likely to fall away from a true center line.

"In a situation like this, trico spinner fall, or almost all spring creek situations, accuracy can make or break an angler's day. Every advantage you have when you start the day adds up. Taking the time to tie good knots as opposed to easy or fast knots can pay off in small percentages that, when added to other minor skills, make you a more efficient angler. Your catch rate will begin to reflect it right away."

Jerry polishes off his sandwich and beer. He takes a deep breath and continues to tell Bobby his philosophy of knots. "Casting skills are essential to accuracy, but why force yourself to make corrections with your cast even if you're not aware of having to make corrections for placement of a fly on a hinged line? Once anglers have tied three surgeon's knots into their leaders, they have essentially put enough turn in the line to rarely be able to hit their targets without some sort of unnecessary correction.

"As far as the question of breaking strength is concerned, the debate goes on whether the blood knot and surgeon's knot are extremely different. The difference may be too subtle to determine whether you'll land a fish. One thing I've learned, though, is that after both knots have been fished and left sitting

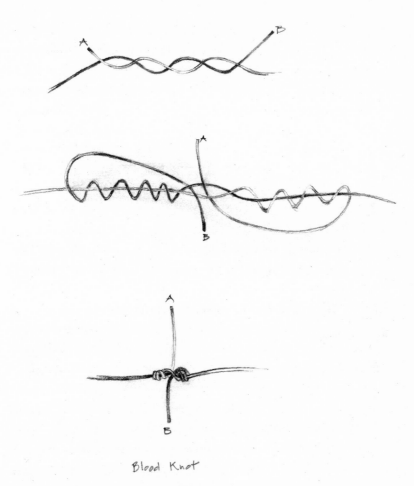

Blood Knot

overnight, the breaking strength of a surgeon's knot significantly decreases while a blood knot seems to be more durable. This is something to keep in mind if you think you're saving time tying a surgeon's knot. In fact, you may be tying more knots more often than you should."

Jerry finishes and gathers up his things. Bobby follows his lead, and they head back down the river. Bobby spies the spot in the run where his other new friend lives, but all is quiet on the water. The sun had risen high, and most of the fish had taken their full bellies to cover, opting for the cool shade and the protection it afforded them.

"I have to leave tomorrow, Jerry," Bobby says. "I want you to know I appreciate your help, and I hope we can fish together again. I know I'll get better by fishing with you, but, to tell the truth, I love the horseradish you put on those roast beef sandwiches."

Jerry laughs out loud. "If you're leaving tomorrow, let's get fishing. I'll show you the blood knot, and you can practice for your next trip out here."

"Thanks, Jerry. I'll be back in the late fall."

The two friends finish up their day on Fairsized Creek by coming across a great spinner fall of golden stoneflies. Jerry is glad to see this event. He had spent the previous week tying patterns for this moment, and now he was going to get to use them. He gives a few to Bobby, and they fish close together as the evening light falls. They talk about families and crazy friends, all the while casting and watching their flies intently. They both hook up to several large fish before dark, but Bobby knows in his gut that the big rainbow from the previous two mornings is going to keep him awake on many nights before he'll get another shot.

"If I get another shot," he mumbles to himself.

CHAPTER 3

THE SECRET OF THE DUN, THE DRY SHAKE, AND THE DUNCAN LOOP

Terrance the trout has grown a full inch bigger over the summer, and autumn is well under way. Today he slides to the very tail of the run with many other smaller trout. Back here the water is flat and glassy. His size allows him to take the best spot in the tailout, which is next to a cut bank. From here Terrance can easily feed but can also duck under the bank at the first bit of disturbance on the glassy surface.

This time of year, the insect of choice for the trout is the fall baetis. Sometimes the trout sit in the tailout for hours before the bugs appear, due to their less-than-predictable hatch time. When they do hatch, they hatch in huge numbers, and it is important that the trout be ready and waiting.

Terrance had managed to get through the summer with only one serious fight for his life, and two near misses. This happened during an above-average grasshopper season, when Terrance was often suckered by well-tied, rubber-legged hopper patterns. These days, hiding out is getting harder and harder to do as water levels drop down to autumn flows. Most of the time Terrance takes shelter in very shallow riffles where hardly anyone can see him. Very few people blind cast into such shallow, turbulent water, and the few that do more often than not reveal their presence by approaching too erect. Terrance had already left the riffles today and is ready to dine in the glide of the run as soon as the insects show.

THE MORNING air is cool and full of falling leaves as Jerry drives out to the county airport to meet Bobby. He left his hounds at home, not wanting to subject them to the cool autumn temperatures. Jerry and Bobby had kept in touch over the last few months, mostly through brief e-mails regarding the progress of Bobby's blood knots. He had his tying time down to less than thirty seconds, and he feels very comfortable with the knot. Jerry warned him that the cool fall days might slow his times a bit due to cold fingers, but everything happens slower this time of year anyway.

Bobby's plane lands right on time, and as soon as hearty hellos are exchanged and bags gathered, the two friends are off for a midday rendezvous with a certain big fish. Jerry turns on the road that goes up the valley and turns down the radio so the two friends can catch up.

"Jerry, how have you been? Thanks a ton for picking me up and depositing me right in the river," Bobby says.

Jerry smiles and replies, "I've been fantastic. My season finished strong, and I'm wealthier and wiser than the last time you saw me. Forget me, though. I gotta tell you, when I saw the size of yesterday's baetis hatch and then saw that big rainbow you were after this summer eating them like they were going out of style, I knew I had to see this match-up again for myself."

"You mean to say you saw that monster eating greedily, and you didn't even throw a line at him?" Bobby responds with a grin and a raised eyebrow.

Jerry grins back and says, "I tell you what—if your plane had been five minutes late coming in today, the urge might have overwhelmed me, but I know you've waited a long time for this shot, and besides, I managed to have quite a day anyway."

"Well, you are truly one of a kind. I'll try not to disappoint," Bobby says. He draws in a deep breath of air from the cracked window and feels the calm of the countryside wash over him.

The two friends are at the stream within minutes. They wader up and string their rods. Bobby cranks out a few nice blood knots in order to change his nine-foot, 4X leader into a twelve-foot, 6X leader. He then ties on the same Adams he had used to imitate the trico in July, and once they are both ready, they quickly stroll upriver. Jerry talks as they walk together.

"Keep this in mind today: The fall baetis the big 'bow is looking for is a busy insect, which, despite the cool weather, writhes and wiggles its little abdomen all over the place as it tries to dry its wings after hatching. It is a fly found on many, many rivers and streams throughout the Americas. After fish have seen substantial pressure during the summer as well as during this particular hatch, they often begin to key in on the movement of the insect. The baetis wiggle despite being able to immediately fly off the water, and the trout find this very appealing. The dilemma for anglers is to make their imitation act like a live mayfly.

"Whole books have been written about making a dry fly come to life, but this is mostly directed toward caddis, stoneflies, and terrestrial insects, using line-twitching and skating techniques. But how does one move a fly's body while keeping it stationary on the water?"

They reach the spot where Jerry had seen the fish earlier in the day, and the baetis are in full swing.

"There he is!" Jerry says and points to the far bank in the tailout.

"Are you sure it's the same fish, Jerry?" Bobby asks. "He is quite a ways back from the eddy where he was feeding this summer."

Jerry confidently responds, "It's the same fish. I know his markings, and I know he's the only twenty-inch fish in this run."

Jerry never finishes what he was saying about the baetis. Bobby is far too excited and heads right to the bank. No more is said. Jerry retires to a log to watch, and Bobby takes up a position straight across from the big rainbow. He watches the fish pick off a few bugs and then begins to cast. He lays beautiful casts down in front of the fish, and he watches as the rainbow consistently takes the naturals all around his fly. Five minutes go by without so much as a look from the big trout, so Bobby stops to take in another deep breath and let the area rest.

TERRANCE HAD been sipping the fall baetis for almost a month now and had quickly learned to target the movement of the insect's abdomen. This was done to prevent the angry insect from showing up. It had worked for him all month, and today is no exception. The afternoon had been easy pickings as each bug struggled, eagerly trying to loosen itself from the surface film of the water. Terrance eats freely until he notices a nice-looking insect, but it drifts without exhibiting any movement at all.

These insects seem to keep showing up in his lane, but Terrance wisely chooses to have nothing to do with such a stationary bug during this hatch.

ANOTHER TEN minutes go by as Bobby repeatedly puts beautiful, straight casts over the big fish. The fish won't spook, but he also won't eat Bobby's imitation. Bobby has waited a long time for this and vows to remain patient. Finally, after a solid fifteen minutes of casting, a twelve-inch rainbow takes Bobby's fly, but it isn't the big fish he was hoping for. The ensuing fight is enough to put the twenty-incher down and makes Bobby shake his head in disbelief. Without turning around and looking at Jerry, Bobby continues to fish up the run, hooking an occasional fish. Once Jerry sees this, he knows it is his cue to venture upstream looking for his own fish, which he does.

After only a couple of casts, Bobby looks upriver and sees Jerry hook his first fish. He watches from a distance as Jerry releases the fish. This scene begins to repeat itself over and over again. One thing Bobby notices is that every time Jerry releases a fish, he goes to his vest.

"Could he be changing flies after every fish?" Bobby wonders.

After Jerry makes a good dozen or so releases in a matter of minutes, Bobby can't stand it any longer. He reels up, hangs his fly on his rod, and heads upriver.

"Got any roast beef?" Bobby yells out.

Jerry turns and smiles. "Are you having some trouble with that fish down there?"

Poker faced, Bobby says, "I'm having trouble with *all* the fish down here, but I can see these fish up here don't have a chance. I figure I can save my pride and ask you over a few pints tonight, or I can step up and ask you right now what the heck you're doing to catch these fish. If nothing else, I can at least go home a little wiser."

Jerry reels up and says, "I put some extra horseradish on yours."

They sit down, and Jerry goes through his vest pockets until he finds his dry shake. He tosses it to Bobby.

"Well, Bobby, if you had stopped and watched before that first cast, you would have noticed that the baetis are full of movement right now. Their abdomens are wiggling like crazy."

Jerry takes his finger and, with a closed fist, wiggles it at Bobby. "It goes like this, and the fish are looking for it. So what I am doing is showing them that my fly has some wiggle, while you show them a fly that is barely moving."

"So how are you wiggling your fly when you're casting up and across without moving the line?" Bobby quickly asks.

"I'm using the three Ds, Bobby. The dun, the dry shake, and the Duncan loop." He takes a deep breath and continues. "The baetis we see today are obviously duns on the water, the newborn winged insect. It is active as heck and needs to be imitated by an active fly. What I do is take a baetis imitation tied in the *thorax* style with an extended body as opposed to a *parachute*-style fly. Then I take the fly and really make it stand on its hackle tips while it's on the water. I do this by using dry-shake floatant material.

"Dry shakes come in many different forms. Choosing one is a matter of preference. A powder with an applicator is usually the best bet, because it allows you to get the floatant well into the fly. Keep in mind, though, that a variety of floatants can be helpful. The gel and liquid fly floatants serve their purpose when you want your fly to leave a bigger impression in the water, such as when you want to imitate spinner falls of large insects like drakes or callibaetis. You can see what kind of impression a fly leaves on the water by looking at its shadow on the bottom of a white bowl. Take a few flies of the same tie and put different types of floatant on all of them, and then put them in a bowl of water. Shine a light over them and look at their corresponding shadows. It will at least give you an idea of how much fly you are showing the fish by using one form of floatant over another. One thing is for certain though: If you want a fly to ride really high, there is no substitute for dry shake. The only downside to dry shake is it's expensive and needs to be reapplied frequently to be effective in the way I use it.

"The last thing I do is tie a Duncan loop into very fine tippet, but I am careful to leave the loop well open. This allows the fly to pivot almost 360 degrees. Any fish that sees a fly with an extended body pivoting on its hackle tips in this fashion has serious difficulty refusing it for the real thing."

Bobby simply stares at Jerry in disbelief. He finally says, "You're kidding, aren't you?"

Jerry is quick to respond. "Not only do I reapply the dry shake after every fish or every three or four casts, I also change the fly once a fish grabs it and use a fresh one. Sometimes I end up with five or six in a drying rotation on my fly patch. After catching a fish, it is also necessary to pull the loop back out of the knot because it will cinch down when you strike the fish."

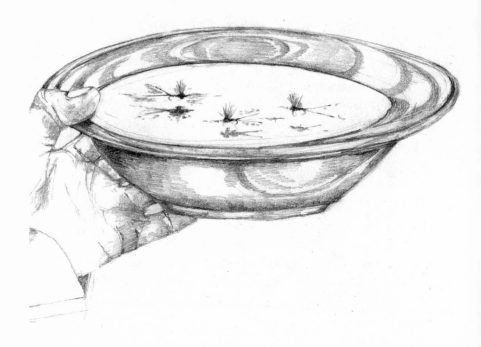

After this last statement, Bobby knows his friend isn't kidding. That is why he had seen Jerry reaching into his vest so much while he was watching from downstream. He was changing flies as well as religiously applying the dry shake and fixing the loop in the knot.

"Wow, Jerry, I must say that is a pretty cool trick, but I don't have any dry shake, and I don't know how to tie the Duncan loop."

Jerry then proceeds to show Bobby the knot and puts some dry shake in a film canister for him as well. The two friends finish their lunch and head upriver. It is late when they come by the big rainbow's run again. The autumn sun had left the water, and

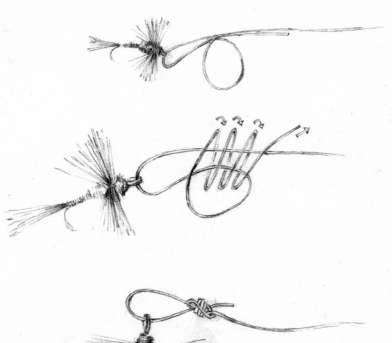

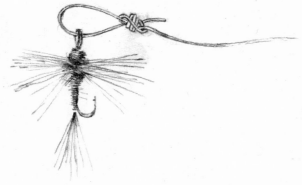

Duncan Loop

the fish are down, with the exception of a few six-inchers that are looking to fatten up on anything before winter's approach.

"Tomorrow, Jerry," Bobby says as they walk by the run on their way to the truck. "Tomorrow the three Ds and I are going to catch that fish. Once again, I thank you for sharing a simple secret with me. You are a fishing saint. Remind me, when we get back to the truck, I've got something for you in return."

It is nearly dark by the time they get out of their gear and into the cab of the truck. Bobby reaches into his bag and pulls out two Cuban cigars. He hands one to Jerry and says, "Don't think life in Big City doesn't come with some perks, my friend."

Jerry smiles and puffs happily on his cigar while the mantra *dun, dry shake, and Duncan loop* plays repeatedly in his head. He is glad to share this knowledge with Bobby. The only thing Jerry likes more than catching fish is to watch someone else get as excited about it as he does, and Bobby definitely does.

CHAPTER 4

FISHING THE CRIPPLE
AND EMERGER

The sun rises steadily the following day, radiating Indian summer heat up and down the Fairsized Creek valley. Bobby had been invited to stay with Jerry on his small farm. Jerry doesn't actually farm the land, but he boards horses and stores other people's cars and boats in his barn. Bobby was sleeping on a couch in front of an oversized woodstove when he is awakened by the sounds of hounds barking outside his window. They feel the morning heat and seem to know that Jerry and Bobby should leave for the river right away.

There is a point near the end of any fishing season when a river seems to let go of all the remaining unhatched insects that it holds—it's as if the insects know that time is getting short. This probably has a lot to do with water temperature and hours of daylight, but no one really knows what exactly goes through a caddis fly's little brain, so the former explanation of the river letting go will have to do.

For whatever reason these glorious late-season days take place, this particular day is going to be one of them, and Jerry feels it when he wakes up. He lets his hounds in for breakfast, knowing this will be enough commotion to wake Bobby. The friends meet on the porch, grabbing boots and waders off the railing and toting along a breakfast of blueberry muffins and bananas to eat on the way to the stream. The back of the truck is filled with nets, rod tubes, vests, waders, and boots. Jerry fires up the truck and shouts to his hounds, "Skeets, Milo, let's go!"

The two hounds come tearing around the corner of the house, knocking one another off balance but pushing on at full speed. They hit the truck bed at full stride, leaping into the air at the same time. There is no way the dogs can skid to a halt on the metal surface at this speed, so they promptly pile into one another in the back of the cab. Which of these four is the most excited this morning is anyone's guess. The anglers quickly double-check the gear, and off they go.

Bobby deeply breathes in the warm morning air. He is glad that Jerry had gotten up early and that they are already heading to the stream. In his haste, though, he had forgotten to brush his teeth, and the taste of yesterday's Cuban cigar lingers. As soon as they get to the stream, Bobby dips his water purifier into Fairsized Creek and takes a long drink. The water is cold and good.

In a matter of moments, Jerry heads upstream several pools. He mumbles something about brook-trout revenge as he leaves, and Bobby doesn't bother to ask what this means. There isn't a lot of apparent insect activity, so Bobby fishes upstream at a slow pace. He searches the water with a Royal Trude, not expecting much action this early in the day. However, it isn't long before he sees his first baetis and first rise of the morning.

THE FALL baetis is on the water in huge numbers by eight in the morning, as the air temperatures had already cleared eighty degrees. Terrance had spent the last few days feeling the extreme temperature changes as well as the shortening daylight hours. Leaves of all colors float overhead all day long. He is well aware that feeding time is getting short and that now is the time to be gluttonous. He had had some close calls with the angry insect over the last few weeks, but Terrance had avoided the hook like an old pro and is constantly growing stronger, bigger, and more educated.

Today Terrance eats baetis emergers as soon as he sees them. The water is warming quickly, and the insect activity is beginning earlier than it had in a week. He quickly switches over to the easier-to-eat duns as soon as they appear in great numbers. This lasts for about fifteen minutes, until Terrance sees a western red quill, a much larger insect. A red quill, a much more satisfying meal compared to the tiny baetis, is floating right down Terrance's lane.

A few days ago Terrance had let the insect slip by. It took about two strong hatches of the red quill before Terrance recognized it as food and locked in on it. Today, though, Terrance expects to see the insect and quickly pursues it for breakfast.

He rises hard to the large mayfly, aggressively smacks it down, and immediately looks for more as he allows hundreds of baetis to float on by.

BOBBY IS still rigged with the previous day's set-up and begins to cast at Terrance as soon as he unstrings his rod. He lays the fly out with confidence. He had dressed it with plenty of dry shake and watches as it seems to dance its way down to the trout.

When the big trout ignores it, Bobby only sighs and casts again. The same result happens on the next six casts. The big trout will not take. Bobby stops casting and watches as the trout continues to aggressively smack the surface. Bobby wishes he could ask Jerry, who is already out of sight, for help. One thing Bobby had learned is that Jerry analyzes his fishing down to the smallest detail. Bobby decides, after he is sure that the fish won't take his offering, to do the same thing. He begins to mull over the situation.

Bobby exits the river, walks well downstream of his targeted trout, and then wades carefully back in. He walks out to where he can see an obvious foam line and stares at it. Multitudes of fall baetis float by, but Bobby diligently watches for any other insect.

Finally, two red quills appear, which are blowing over the surface and fighting to lift off the water. He watches as a four-inch rainbow frantically chases one of the two flies. The little trout successfully snatches the huge insect and immediately vanishes to the river bottom.

Bobby looks up to where his big trout is feeding and for the first time notices that the fish is really moving from side to side for quite some distance. He concludes correctly that the fish is looking for the bigger, although more scarce, bug. In a matter of moments, even before Bobby can tie on a new fly and get into position, the red quills begin to hatch by the hundreds. It is as if a switch has been thrown. Western red quills appear everywhere.

Terrance can't get enough. He eats greedily, moving upstream a few feet to get insects, and then swims back to his starting point. He eats his way upriver like this again and again. The wind has picked up, and many of the quills are beginning to blow and skate sideways toward the bank. Terrance doesn't bother to chase them down; instead, he begins to eat only the emergers and cripples that are stuck in the water and can't be skated by the wind. There are so many bugs hatching, these easy targets are not hard to find. He slows his pace as he eats more deliberately while looking for the cripples.

Bobby ties on a size 14 Quill Gordon and false casts over Terrance. He makes a nice presentation, does a good upstream line mend, and puts the fly right in front of the big trout. The fish rises, but not to Bobby's fly.

Bobby lifts the fly and casts again. Same mend, same drift, same result.

"There are just too many naturals," Bobby says aloud to himself.

He casts again and again. The trout doesn't spook, but it never even looks at his fly.

Bobby again speaks out loud to himself. "What could I possibly be doing wrong this time?"

On cue, Bobby hears a familiar voice behind him.

"He's probably eating the emerger."

Bobby looks back and sees Jerry comfortably seated on his usual log. He asks Jerry how long he's been there.

"Long enough to notice that not one of those red quill duns has been eaten since I sat down."

"So that's it? If the fish are not on the dun but are on the quill, they must be on the cripples and stillborn insects. So all I have to do is put a big cripple pattern on, right?" Bobby asks.

Jerry rises, walks toward Bobby, and says, "Go ahead and tie on a cripple, and then let me see it before you show it to that fish."

Jerry checks the tippet on Bobby's leader to make sure he had bulked it up a bit from what he had used on the little fall baetis. As Bobby searches his boxes for his biggest cripple patterns, Jerry reminds him to make sure his tippet diameter is able to hold a heavier-gauge hook without breaking.

"How do I do that?" Bobby asks.

Jerry shakes his head and smiles. "Well, I have always pulled on my knots after I tie them to see if the breaking strength is okay."

Bobby shakes his head and also smiles. "Dumb question, I guess."

"Not really," Jerry replies.

BRIGHT YELLOW leaves from hillside aspens light on the water, drift with the insects, and foam over Terrance's head. He takes no notice of the leaves; he only knows that one thing is better to eat than the other. The sun had warmed the valley air, and the afternoon winds are beginning to pick up. Fall had certainly arrived on Fairsized Creek, and every valley resident, from fish to deer to the local snowplow operator, is preparing for winter.

BOBBY FINDS the fly he wants. It is a leftover Green Drake Cripple from the spring. He ties an improved clinch knot, dresses the top of the fly with floatant, tugs on the knot, and hands it to Jerry.

"The reason that was not a dumb question, Bobby," Jerry says, "is because I don't use an improved clinch knot on this fly. What you want to use is the knot you just learned."

"You mean the Duncan loop?" Bobby asks.

"Yep, and do you know why?" Jerry replies.

Bobby inhales deeply. "You know, I don't, but I have a feeling you're going to tell me."

They both laugh.

"Yes, I am going to tell you, and if you're going to feel bad about it, go ahead and send me a check in the mail, or better yet, have your people call my people and work something out."

Bobby butts in, "I would, but your people are two hounds named Skeets and Milo."

Jerry rolls his eyes and smiles. "In this case, your question wasn't dumb because you don't want to pull your loop tight on this knot. In regard to the cripple pattern, the Duncan loop or other loop knot should be the knot of choice. This is because the cripple pattern is tied a particular way in order to be fished a particular way. That is, hook bend down and eye of the hook up. This will make the fly appear to be a true cripple, half submerged and half emerged. I want you to look hard at the clinch knot you just tied there, Bobby, and see how the fly is forced to ride after the knot has been tightened down."

Bobby takes a look and responds, "I see what you mean. The hook shank is going to ride horizontally on the water instead of vertically in the water, half submerged no matter how I dress the fly. The influence of the knot is overriding the way the fly should be sitting."

"I don't need to tell you, Bobby, but when you false cast, your fly gets dried off in the air. In the case of a cripple this is bad, because you're constantly drying the end of the fly that you want to sink. You're going to need a knot that will allow the fly to hang freely in the water yet retain its breaking strength, which the Duncan loop does nicely. It is also important that you keep

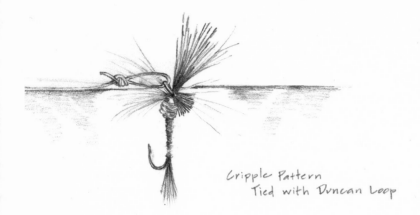

Cripple Pattern
  Tied with Duncan Loop

Cripple Pattern
Tied with Clinch
  Knot

your false casts to a minimum so the rear of the fly stays good and saturated with water, and because of this, I recommend you use a dry shake on the post of the fly and reapply it frequently to keep the top of the fly very buoyant and visible. Brands of dry shake that come with brush applicators are usually the best for dressing cripples, because you can apply it to the areas of the fly you want as opposed to shaking the whole fly."

Bobby smiles and reties his knot. When he finishes, he looks at Jerry and shakes his head. "You don't miss a beat, do you?"

Jerry responds with a smile. Bobby puts the dry-shake floatant on the top of the cripple and uses his saliva to sink the rear. He then once again strips line off his reel. He can still see the big rainbow rising strong directly across the stream.

Jerry is sitting down again by the time Bobby begins to false cast. Bobby gets the distance he wants and then shoots his line and fly over the riffles of the run. The line and fly join the medley of falling aspen leaves and lightly fall to the water. The fly lands a good five feet above the trout, which is good for Bobby, giving the fly an extra second or two to settle into its proper riding position.

The big fish eats once, twice, and then slides right up to Bobby's Green Drake pattern. The fly is the right size and is riding perfectly, and the fish can only do one thing: It inhales the offering.

Bobby sees it happen and reacts perfectly. For a mere second Bobby's fly rod arcs forward like a crescent moon. Then, just as quickly, the rod straightens as the fish leaves the water. There is nothing Bobby can do.

TERRANCE HAD done it again. The angry insect is back, and Terrance the trout knows instantly what he has done. His response is instantaneous. He leaps powerfully from the water, his momentum carries him over into a back flip, and the fly lets go. Terrance crashes back into the water and dives for the depths of the run, freed again from a bad mouthful. He won't rise or move out of the depths anytime soon.

BOBBY IS shocked when he sees his line and fly hurtling back toward him as the trout leaves the water. This is the first time Bobby has fully seen the mass of this huge rainbow. "That fish is way bigger than I thought he was," thinks Bobby as he ducks the line and fly.

He watches as the water flies up from the trout's downward impact. He sees a flash in the depths, and then, stunned, he blinks and looks around. He turns and says to Jerry, "Did you see that?"

"Absolutely," Jerry responds. "That was really awesome. I can't believe the size of that fish. I think it's fair to say you made him a bit mad."

Bobby is torn between his happiness over finally hooking the wily rainbow and his sorrow over losing him so quickly, and Jerry can sense this. Jerry can't think of anything to say that will console Bobby, so he says the only thing he can think of. "Do you want a roast beef sandwich, Bobby?"

Bobby reels up his line, and as he does, his emotions settle on the side of happiness. His goal had been to fool that fish, and he had done it. He had needed some help, but he had been willing to learn, and his patience paid off.

Over a sandwich and a river-temperature beer, Jerry reassures Bobby that he will again get another shot at the huge rainbow, but before that can happen Bobby has to go with Jerry to a little-known spring creek for a day. It is called Grassy Brook and is about two valleys west of Fairsized Creek.

Jerry tells Bobby that tomorrow is his birthday, and a friend of a friend had gotten him some access on the water, which was on a large working cattle ranch. Jerry is allowed to bring one friend and asks Bobby if he'd like to go. Jerry tells Bobby that he had fished there a lot as a child but hadn't been back since. It is going to be something special for both of them: a reunion of sorts for Jerry and a chance to fish rarely accessible virgin water for Bobby.

CHAPTER 5

SKIP AN X

The washboard surface of the road rattles every screw and nut holding Jerry's old pickup together. The years of dirt, rust, and grime somehow keep the parts tightly welded, though, and the old truck rambles on. In the back, Jerry's hounds run from side to side looking for passing varmints, and in the cab sit two men whose teeth have never rattled so hard and who have never been so happy about it.

After a few strong pulls on his coffee, Bobby eases down into the seat of the pickup and asks Jerry what he remembers about fishing on Grassy Brook. Jerry looks up at his windshield visor. There, hanging upside down, is a tattered Dave's Hopper that instantly makes him smile.

"What I remember most, Bobby, is exactly what the name of the place implies. It's a small piece of water with very grassy banks. The fish I used to catch there were always tucking themselves up under the grassy overhangs. There were always good hatches there as well. The combination made for some big fish in small water, and even though the angling pressure there was always light, the degree of difficulty was always appealing."

Jerry tells story after story about different fish he had caught there. Some were lunkers, others hogs; some were pigs and footballs; and, of course, the monster fish surpassed all these.

Bobby listens and becomes more excited with each passing tale of fish and fishing. The sun rises a little higher and warms the valley floor where the little brook runs. With the warmth comes a steady breeze, which rapidly, to the great dismay of Jerry and Bobby, increases in speed until it becomes a howling wind.

As Jerry eases the truck into the ranch entrance, leaves of every color fly by the windows. The two friends peer out at the ominous conditions, but neither angler's spirit will be dampened on this day. They check in with one of the ranch hands and then head through a large pasture toward Grassy Brook. To the credit of the ranchers, the brook is fenced from the cattle except for two drinking areas. Jerry is excited when he sees the brook again for the first time in a long time.

"I can't believe it; not a thing has changed. It is exactly how I remember it, Bobby."

Bobby surveys the scene and notices several large fish rising on the far bank. They are just as Jerry had said, tucked under overhanging grass and feeding aggressively on a small mayfly spinner.

"Look over there. Those spinning mayflies are using the grass as a windbreak, and there are a few nice fish sucking them down as they die and fall in the water."

Jerry steps forward and looks. "Yes, sir, you're right. That's just what I was hoping to see. Let's grab our rods and fish this bank together."

Bobby is already rigging up as Jerry says this. He asks Jerry if they should wear waders, but Jerry says the brook is really a bank fishery. That is good enough for Bobby. The two men dress their flies and approach the water.

The wind is sharp and blowing directly at them. Jerry casts and drops the fly perfectly under the grass, which overhangs the water and the fish by a foot or so. He sees a large head poke up and take his offering. He sets the hook, and water begins to fly.

He releases the fish a few moments later and yells over to Bobby, who is false casting for the third time to the far bank.

"Hey, Bobby, did you happen to hear the birthday song my reel was just singing to me?"

Bobby doesn't turn his gaze from the far bank but yells back that he had heard plenty. His fly lands on the water but is a foot and sometimes even two feet short of where he needs it to be. The wind is crippling the leader and tippet right at the end of the cast. He stops casting as Jerry fights another big trout. Shortening the leader is an option, but this will bring the tippet diameter up too much for such a gentle stream. He could make it short and light, but he had already been warned by Jerry that a long leader is necessary here to keep the fish from hearing the smack of the fly line on the water. These trout are under the grassy overhangs for a reason: The meadow simply has no cover. There are no trees, no willow bushes—nothing but grass. This makes the trout very wary of streamside predators, and they constantly stay on guard, aware of noises in the water and any vibrations around them. If they sense anything wrong, the fish will surely disappear completely under the banks.

Bobby watches Jerry land a nice twenty-inch fish and in the process notices that Jerry's leader is at least twelve feet long. So he pays attention as Jerry casts, assuming it must be a technique that

Jerry is employing that Bobby isn't, especially in these extremely windy conditions. What he sees is a relatively gentle cast, low to the water with a nice straight leader extending out and finishing off with the fly landing softly on the water under the grass.

"Jerry, how come I'm a foot short on every cast?" Bobby yells over the wind.

"Are you keeping the line close to the water when you cast?" Jerry hollers back without missing a beat, as he delivers yet another perfect cast.

"Yes, I think it's plenty low," Bobby says.

Jerry strikes and hooks another fish, and as he does he finally looks toward Bobby. "Skip an X!" Jerry says and resumes fighting his fish.

Bobby is left to figure it out this time, but with this clue he kneels in the grass, peers into the river, and begins to think it over. If a person were to skip an X, let's say tying 3X tippet into 5X tippet with a blood knot, would the breaking strength be strong enough to hold a fish? Well, it must be since Jerry bothered to mention it. Something to keep in mind, though, is Jerry always uses very soft rods, which he swears by. He believes he can land bigger fish with softer rods because of their shock-absorption qualities. The "bend potential," as Jerry likes to call it, is what protects his light tippets from breaking. He says he is never afraid to red line his rod on a big fish. Marry this knowledge together with how many fish Jerry had fought and all he knows about confusing a fish to hand rather than wearing him down, and you have a serious advantage on the river.

Bobby pulls two feet of 4X from his tippet spool and then pulls an equal amount of 6X. He ties the two together with a blood knot and pulls. He is surprised at how well they hold. Next he snips off the 4X and tries tying 3X to 6X tippet. Again, the blood knot holds very well.

It becomes obvious to Bobby almost immediately what to do: He will build a new twelve-foot leader. This time he makes his taper heavy and long, so that by the time he is eleven feet into the taper, his end diameter is at 3X. To this he ties a foot of 6X tippet and a fly. The wind riffles on the water are enough to cover a splashy landing that the heavy leader might cause. Bobby is satisfied with his new set-up. He chooses the biggest head he can see under the grass across from him and begins to cast.

The leader cuts through the wind, and the loop unfolds nicely. The one-foot section of 6X piles up under the grass like a mini parachute cast. Bobby is on target, and the fly had floated about nine inches when suddenly the water under the grass becomes white and flies through the air in every direction. The fish is on, and Bobby knows he has to back off this fish until it settles down. He eases the pressure, and the fish runs a short distance downstream and then holds.

At this point Bobby does what he has seen Jerry do to fish dozens of times. He keeps his rod pointed high and pulls the fish to one side until the fish adjusts to the direction of the pull, then he instantly turns the rod and pulls the fish the other way. Every time the fish makes the adjustment against the pressure, the rod is rocked in the other direction and some line is gained. In a matter of moments, the fish doesn't know which way to swim, and Bobby pulls him close enough to net him. It is a bright fifteen-inch cuttbow. He gently releases the fish and looks for another target.

Bobby catches and releases one more nice fish before he decides to retie his 6X tippet knot, just to ensure its breaking strength. This turns out to be a great technique for him, because Bobby finishes the day by releasing fourteen rainbows more than fifteen inches long. He only breaks off one fish, which he is sure would have broken off even if he had tied his fly to a tire chain. Bobby makes a conscious effort to set his leader up differently with every bank he fishes, depending on what he thinks the wind direction and conditions call for. He has unglued himself from the idea that there is a single right way to set up a leader. From this moment on, Bobby understands that his leaders are going to work for him and not against him. He has come a long way with knot-tying speed and efficiency, and today his catch shows it.

Looking across the darkening field, Bobby can see the dim flash of Jerry's headlights. This is the signal to wrap it up. Bobby thinks back on the day. When had he and Jerry split up? No matter, he thinks. The evening air is unusually warm, and Bobby's soul is feeling equally warm. He swings his rod tip behind him and walks to Jerry's truck.

CHAPTER 6

UNDERSTANDING AND USING PROPER TIPPET DIAMETERS

Today is Bobby's last day on the water for a while, and he will gratefully be spending it with his friend Jerry. Bobby feels that he's gained some measure of respect from Jerry after fishing yesterday. The hint Jerry gave him, as opposed to the solution, had set him free to choose from the endless array of leader possibilities. Instead of being confined to one fix or particular set-up, Bobby could now set his leader up to what the situation dictated. He feels good that Jerry thought enough of him to let him figure it out on his own, which he did with much success. Jerry isn't here to take pity or take Bobby under his wing; he is just here to fish and likes Bobby's company. That suits Bobby perfectly.

They decide to start with breakfast at a nearby diner called Chuck's Roost that is known for tire-size flapjacks.

"One last day on Fairsized Creek before the snow falls, huh Bobby?" Jerry says. He speaks with the bottom of his beard dimpling the syrup on his plate, while he shoves a forkful of flapjacks into his mouth.

Bobby can only chuckle at this display. It would be useless to tell Jerry about the syrup on his chin, because Jerry would surely say something about saving it for later.

Bobby says to Jerry, "I think a nice short day on our fair little creek is in order. They said on the radio that the high today will only reach forty-five degrees. That's a pretty drastic change from the Indian summer we had yesterday. The mountains certainly have a way of making their own weather. I bet it's going to shut the bugs down a bit."

Jerry mutters something through a mouthful of pancake and syrup. Bobby can't exactly hear Jerry but can tell it is a response of agreement. He then leans over his plate and fills up on hot dough, butter, and syrup. The waitress keeps the coffee topped off, and they drink plenty of it. When they're finished, they settle up the bill and waddle toward the door, talking about the effects of weather on football and elk bugling. They swap stories all the way to the river.

Like Bobby had predicted, there isn't a whole lot of visible activity on the water when they arrive. It is late enough in the season and the temperatures are cold enough for Jerry to decide to rig a large H and L variant with a size 16 Bead-Head Pheasant-Tail Nymph as a dropper. In past years Jerry had seen plenty of big heads rise slowly and engulf the big dry fly under these same conditions, but Jerry knows that the money fly in this case will be the Pheasant Tail. He takes great care to pick a good one from his fly box. This particular one is a Bead-Head, Flash-Back Pheasant Tail.

Bobby follows Jerry's lead and rigs a Royal Wulff with a pheasant tail as well. His fly selection is fine for the conditions, but Bobby had overlooked one minor detail.

The trout in Fairsized Creek are quite stunned by the cold waters this morning and, due to little or no bug activity, are conserving their energy. They sit in the slowest currents, whether

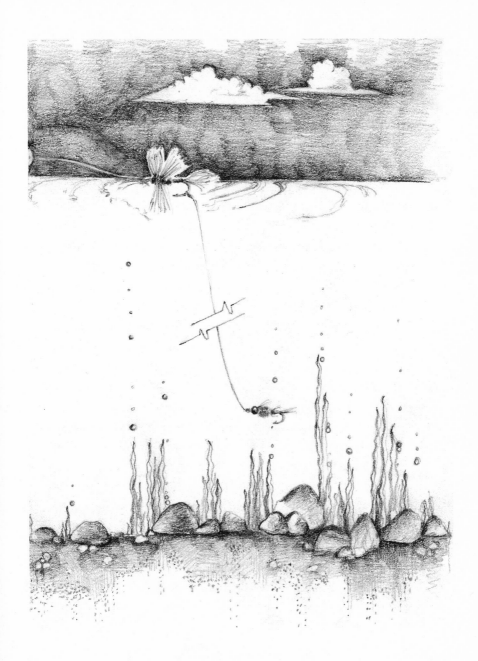

this means close to the bank, behind structure, or on the bottom. In any case, none of them are going to travel any great distance for a small meal. Any meal that they are going to eat is going to have to be right in front of their faces, or it will be ignored as a potential waste of energy.

Bobby steps into the water first and begins fishing upstream at a decent pace. Jerry starts behind his friend and follows him on up. They concentrate on the slow riffle in the middle of the day's first run, sensing that this is where the most fish will congregate.

It isn't long before Jerry hooks up on his dropper fly. Bobby anticipates a strike on his fly at any moment. The fishing conditions aren't perfect, but it is turning into a great day to be outside. Bobby is so lost in the blue skies and sunshine that he is mildly startled by his first hook-up of the day. This had not taken long, but Jerry had already released four fish of varying size by the time Bobby had hooked his first one. The two friends continue to work upstream for two more good runs together, and Bobby notices that Jerry is still catching more fish.

Bobby understands that he isn't quite the fly angler Jerry is, but he is using the same set-up in the same runs, and he is still being outfished four to one, even though he is fishing through the runs first. Bobby wonders if it could be that the fish are leader shy. When he set up his lead fly and dropper, he had tied the tippet down to 4X, and then he proceeded to tie an extra two-foot length of 4X tippet to the hook shank of his lead fly. He then tied the Bead-Head Pheasant Tail to the tag end of the tippet coming from the dry fly. He had pulled on all the knots and felt comfortable with this set-up.

Bobby switches his nymph patterns in order to find a solution, but the results remain the same, with Jerry constantly cleaning up behind him. Finally he can take it no longer. The waitress at the diner had supplied the two anglers with roast beef sandwiches, and Bobby suggests that it might be time for one.

Jerry agrees. He senses the frustration in his friend's voice, but he isn't worried. He's pretty sure that he already knows what the trouble is, and it's an easy fix. Jerry asks Bobby specifically how he set up his leader and dropper, so Bobby tells him.

"Bobby," Jerry said, "you just missed a simple step. You're not getting deep enough, quick enough, with your nymph. Let me ask you this: Were almost all the fish you caught at the end of your drift, or as you lifted the fly for your next cast?"

"Yes, now that you mention it, they were," Bobby responds. "But I watched how much tippet you had from your dry fly to your dropper, and I must be at least as deep as you."

Jerry frees his sandwich from a well-folded piece of wax paper and says, "The key is to make your fly go deep quickly, so that the majority of your drift is near the bottom where you're targeting the fish. In fly fishing the art of casting weighty set-ups becomes akin to playing volleyball with a football; it's the same sport, but some of the fun is gone. So in order to use the least weight possible, in this case a single bead-head fly, but still fish it effectively, it is important to think about how your tippet acts on the fly as gravity tries to pull it to the bottom. Your tippet has a certain amount of buoyancy that keeps it from sinking easily. What is more important, though, is the line diameter and its resistance in the water caused by the friction of the line being pulled through the water's depths. The thicker the diameter, the slower the line can drop through the water. A thinner filament has less resistance and is pulled down by the fly easier. The point is, a tippet diameter sometimes shouldn't be chosen based on landing a fish of a certain size, or because you're worrying about a leader-shy fish. Sometimes how quickly a line can sink should be a deciding factor when choosing tippet size.

"The idea of sink rates of different tippet diameters is amplified even more by the speed of the current. So when it comes to dropping the nymph into a particular zone, you have to take into account the time needed for the fly to sink as well as the distance needed upstream in order for the fly to have time to sink to the desired depth."

Jerry begins to eat his sandwich, and Bobby tries to finish Jerry's thoughts. "So the shorter my cast, and the swifter the current, the less time I'm spending with my fly in the fish's zone. But if I were to lengthen my cast as much as possible and drop my tippet diameter to my nymph so the fly can pull the line down more efficiently, even though I might not need a small tippet due to leader-shy fish, I may need one just to help my fly get into position without opening up my split-shot container. The only other consideration is the minimum tippet diameter I can use that won't leave me decorating fish with my hooks."

Jerry responds, "You can take this one step further when you think about strike-indicator fishing with a nymph, or a pair of nymphs. Think about the last few days and how you have been playing with various leader set-ups. Next time you're fishing deep on a cold day, or whenever you think you should be deep, consider your leader. Try a heavy taper all the way to the strike indicator, and then dramatically lighten the taper to the fly, to a strength you feel comfortable landing the fish with, but no more and no less. This will drop your fly to the bottom in a hurry and enables you to get more depth with less casting distance upstream. If you were to try and switch to a dry fly with this set-up, it probably wouldn't cast well at all, but with the weight of the nymph to help straighten out the leader it should work just fine for a deep-water set-up.

"I suppose what I'm trying to say is this: When you're dry-fly fishing, consciously set up your leader for casting, but when you're nymph fishing, consciously set up your leader for drifting. Then see what happens to your catch rate."

By the time Jerry had finished speaking, Bobby had already rerigged his nymph with lighter tippet. Then the two men head off to another access on Fairsized Creek.

Bobby catches many more fish by the end of the day, and he vows to always think about the minor details when he takes to the water in the future. After changing from their waders, Jerry and Bobby drive to the airport. On the way there they discuss the upcoming winter fishing. Bobby will be back after New Year's to visit for a couple of weeks. The next time he steps into Fairsized Creek, snow will line its borders, and getting ice stuck in the rod guides will be the norm. He can't wait.

The two friends shake hands at the airport entrance, Jerry's hounds bellow their good-byes, and about twenty minutes later, with Bobby in the air and Jerry snoring in front of a football game, it begins to snow.

WINTER IS upon the valley of Fairsized Creek, and Terrance the trout is well aware of this. He had moved with many other fish to the deepest, slowest confines of the pool. The aggression of the fish is at a minimum since there are few, if any, insects to fight over, and none of the fish want to expend the energy to fight over space. About every third day a light midge hatch develops, despite the cold temperatures. Most of the fish rise to them in the back eddy or in the slow riffles near the center of the run. Terrance prefers the back eddy due to the extra protection it seems to offer from the angry insect.

It is a nice bonus for the fish when the midges show up. The hatch will increase in frequency as the winter bears on, but for now the fish spend about 90 percent of their time sitting still and using very little energy.

About the same time Bobby steps off his plane that day and Jerry stirs from his nap, Terrance successfully outwaits a large stonefly nymph that is trying to pass from one streambed cobble to another. Terrance will stay big and healthy despite winter's grip on his home.

CHAPTER 7

THE LOST ART OF
SWINGING FLIES

There is four feet of snow on the banks of Fairsized Creek by the time Bobby returns to the valley in late January. He gathers his baggage and is somewhat surprised that Jerry has not shown up at the airport. That had been the plan two days ago when they last spoke. Then again, it is snowing quite hard. Bobby thinks that maybe Jerry didn't want to risk the drive in his old truck, or, worse yet, he could have tried to get to the airport and gotten stuck in the snow somewhere.

Bobby waits about twenty minutes and then decides that the best thing to do is take a cab to Jerry's house, following the most likely route in case the latter prediction is correct. Sure enough, the roads are bad, but there's no sign of Jerry's truck in a ditch or snowbank. Twenty minutes later the cab pulls in to Jerry's long driveway and drives down toward the farmhouse. Bobby notices that there is a lack of gravel crunching under the tires. He never realized how much he associates that noise with the good times he's had since he met his new friend, but with the snow pack the ride is eerily quiet. Bobby is more than a little worried about Jerry.

Through the front window of the farmhouse, Bobby can make out a hound staring back at him. He knows that if Skeets and Milo are in the front room Jerry has to be home. The truck is surely in the barn. Bobby sends the cab off, walks to the door, and knocks. There is no answer, so Bobby tries the knob. It is unlocked, and he lets himself in.

"Hello, Jerry? Anyone home? Any fly anglers living in here?" Bobby tries to cut the tension he feels with humor, but it doesn't ease his mind. The hounds are instantly upon him, leaping up and down in excitement to see their fishing pal, but there is still no response from Jerry. He lets the dogs outside and listens.

Then Bobby thinks he hears something coming from the next room. It is a thudding sound coming from the back of the kitchen. Bobby thinks he can hear a muffled voice but isn't sure.

He concentrates harder on the noise. He's sure of it now—it is pounding. He walks slowly in the direction of the noise. He reaches for the kitchen light, but the power is out. Bobby can make out a shadow in the back of the kitchen, and apparently the pounding is coming from there. He approaches slowly, and as he comes closer he can see that the dark shape on the floor is a cellar entrance, with two flat doors facing up at him. The pounding is coming from the other side of these doors. Bobby reaches down and pulls the left door open.

As the door swings open, something quickly flies by Bobby's head, straight up from the cellar. Bobby swings his hand out to fend off what he suddenly realizes is a tennis ball. He looks down, and in the dim light of a cellar window that Jerry had painted shut, he sees his friend staring up at him. In one hand Jerry holds a tennis racket, and in the other is a black box. The cellar ladder, which Jerry had built himself out of local lodgepole pine, lays at his feet in pieces.

"Thank heaven, you're here at last. I could have spent the winter down here!" Jerry is obviously very glad to see his friend and was hoping Bobby would show up soon to help him.

Bobby responds, "Well, at least you store most of your canned goods down there."

Jerry can only laugh at his own predicament. Before Bobby will rescue him, though, Jerry has to say three times that Bobby is the better fly angler. Laughing, Bobby retrieves a ladder from the barn so Jerry can climb out.

As it turns out, Jerry had gone down to flip the fuses when the power went out and never made it back to the kitchen. He had spent two hours repeatedly hitting a tennis ball against the cellar doors, hoping that Bobby would soon come and hear it. However, while he was down there he had not only found his father's old wood tennis racquet, but his grandfather's old fly box as well.

The box is stuffed with nymphs of every size. They seem reasonably intact and surprisingly up-to-date. Expecting to see wet flies of a more traditional, fancy type, both Jerry and Bobby are shocked to see flies that look like they were bought at the local fly shop two days ago. Both men round up candles from various rooms in the house. Jerry fires up the woodstove and lets the hounds back in. Meanwhile, Bobby is mesmerized by the old fly box.

"You know, Bobby, there is a story behind that fly box. My father told it to me when I was little, and I had forgotten about it until I saw that box tonight. As I was hitting that tennis ball for the last two hours I was able to remember the whole story. Would you like to hear it?"

Bobby smiles and says, "Is this the old ghost-story-by-the-fire routine?"

"No, honestly, this is supposedly a true story and is the reason why that box exists today." Jerry sounds very sincere. The coffee is warming on the woodstove, the lights are out, and the storm is on—it's a good time for a tale.

"Tell me the story, Jerry," Bobby says as he eases back into his chair. Skeets and Milo come in to the room and lay down in front of the stove, seemingly ready to hear the tale as well.

The smell of burning wood, steaming coffee, and wet bloodhound fills the room. Bobby finds himself in a state of pure Rocky Mountain intoxication as Jerry begins his story.

"My grandfather was a boy of the West who grew up in Oregon. His father worked at timber, and his mother worked at keeping them happy and healthy. My grandfather, whose name was Martin, was free to roam the expansive countryside. He soon learned that what he enjoyed most was fishing. Whether it was catching salmon in the smallest of rivers or trying to manipulate sturgeon with chicken gizzards, Martin loved fishing. By the time he was eleven Martin was an accomplished angler, and on his twelfth birthday he was given a cane fly rod and that wood box."

Jerry points at the box full of flies that Bobby is methodically turning over and over in his hands. Jerry inhales deeply and continues.

"Martin had only seen an angler fly fish once before, so he was forced to teach himself what to do solely based on that memory. The box he was given had come wrapped in a single leaflet of paper. The paper had shown a few fly patterns and a drawing of a man that was labeled, SIR ALFRED THAMES, THE GREATEST ENGLISH FLY ANGLER ALIVE TODAY. To Martin this was ridiculous. He knew there was no Sir Alfred Thames just as surely as there were no fairies in his mother's garden. Nonetheless, he copied the flies on the page as best he could with feathers from local chicken stocks and upland game he shot after school. He then began to fly fish with a lot of vigor, but with little to no success.

"My grandfather was stubborn, though, and the worse he did fly fishing, the more obsessed he became to learn everything there was about it. Months went by, and Martin hadn't caught a single fish. Finally, a year went by, and Martin's grand total for one year of fly fishing was exactly one fish. He began to think that fly fishing wasn't meant for those Northwest woods.

"It wasn't until my grandfather was in school the following year that he figured some things out about fly fishing. This was due to a little help from a local boy named Nathaniel Logan. The kids in school called him Woodsy because Nathaniel's family lived the farthest away from the school. They had a small farm right at the edge of woods that, for all intents and purposes, were uninhabited. Anyway, one day Martin and Woodsy were held after school because they'd had a minor scuffle during lunch. Even though they had scraped and bruised one another pretty effectively, vying for the attention of a new little girl in their class, they nonetheless got to talking about the simple after-school pleasures they were missing that day. Somehow Martin had let his secret of fly fishing failure slip. He wasn't too worried, though, thinking that Woodsy wouldn't know what fly fishing was anyway.

"It turns out that he couldn't have been more wrong. Woodsy had practically grown up in the rivers and lakes near his house and had only fished with fly rods from his earliest memory. A bond was quickly formed between the boys, and they agreed to meet at the creek nearest Woodsy's home early the following Saturday morning.

"Well, Saturday came around, and Martin awoke to sheets of Oregon rain pouring from the sky. He dressed carefully in order to stay dry as long as possible. He grabbed his gear and ran toward Woodsy's. It was a good four-mile run through farm fields and thinned woods, but Martin made it just as Woodsy showed up. The two new friends stood in the rain as Woodsy quickly showed my grandfather a variety of knots, which he was supposed to tie. Martin began on the knots while Woodsy disappeared up the river with his rod in hand.

"Martin stood in that rain for nearly an hour trying to tie those knots. He had never seen knots like these before, but he took his time and did it right. He was soaked to the bone but warm with ambition inside. He walked up the river to find Woodsy and see what was next.

"They found one another, and after Woodsy had confirmed that Martin had taught himself to cast well enough, he pointed at a large rock sticking out of the middle of the river. He announced to Martin that they were going to get on that rock. Since they were both soaked through, walking in the water wasn't going to make much difference. They didn't hesitate a moment and were both seated on the boulder within minutes. Then Nathaniel 'Woodsy' Logan told my grandfather, 'Martin, what I'm going to show you with the line and rod others know, but what I will show you in the river is what the fish told me alone, as far as I know.'

"With that he showed my grandfather the art of swinging a nymph through the water. Fishing the fly on the tight line was one of the main ways to fish a nymph before the advent of the strike indicator.

"Anglers had been fishing wet flies for ages on a tight line and catching fish with traditional wet-fly patterns, but Woodsy had met a man one day. According to Woodsy, the man's name was Mister Rhead. He'd met this man while fishing in these parts when Woodsy was only nine years old. One afternoon Mr. Rhead had filled his head with the idea of fishing imitative flies, like stoneflies and rock worms, for trout. The flies most people used were fancy flies, but Mr. Rhead was right—showing fish imitations of aquatic insects at certain times of year was an unbelievable way to fish. Woodsy began to catch more fish than ever.

"The next thing Mr. Rhead showed Martin was the fly he was casting. Woodsy took a fly from his fly box and held it up like it was a grail. It looked to Martin like some sort of roach. It was large, brown, and roughly oval shaped. The material looked like horsehair. This fly apparently sunk since there was no hackle to keep it from doing so.

"Woodsy cast directly across the river and let his fly settle for a moment. He then took an enormous upstream mend, dropped his rod tip to the water, delicately gripped the rod above the cork with two fingers, and proceeded to follow the line with his rod tip as the line swung across the current below him. About halfway through the swing of the line, Woodsy lifted quickly, but not hard, actually letting a little bit of line slip as he lifted. He tightened the line and set the hook. A big rainbow leapt through the air, and Woodsy deftly fought and landed it. Now it was Martin's turn.

"Martin took the strange fly from Woodsy and cast it across the river to where his friend had just cast. He made a mend, and the fly began to sink and drift downstream. He felt the fly tap on the line as the slack ran out and the line became tight. Then the fly began swinging across the river below him.

"The rain pounded down around him, but Martin was locked in on this one thing, this one moment in time, and a tsunami wouldn't have distracted him now. The line swung below him and began to slow; nothing had struck. Martin began to lift for another cast when suddenly his rod buckled in half. Martin's instinct was to strike, which he did with a vengeance, and then it was over. The line had broken like it was nothing. Martin had blown it.

"Suddenly, through the sound of the pounding rain, Martin could hear something else: Woodsy laughing.

"'Oh, that was great!' Woodsy howled between tears. 'You should have seen your face!'

"Martin wasn't sure he saw the humor in all of this, but he instantly felt a little better when Woodsy relaxed and gave him another fly. First he told my grandfather this:

"My daddy used to work on one of the first submarines. The only thing he ever gave me before his submarine sank was a submariner's underwater mask for looking at keels and such. Well, one day I took it from my shelf, grabbed an old garden hose, and came down to this big fishing hole near my house. I went to the bottom while breathing through the garden hose.

I could stay down quite a while before I got too cold. After a while the fish weren't scared of me. I sat and watched as they ate the bugs underwater and especially the bugs that were moving. That is when I also noticed that there were literally thousands of stonefly nymphs in this particular stream. That's when I decided to try and catch fish like this, like Mr. Rhead had said to do it. It became the only way I liked to fish.

"Now let me tell you why it works so well, Martin. What happens is this: Your fly is good and buggy looking, and when you cast across the river and mend the line, the fly sinks to the bottom, and when that line comes tight with the current below you, the fly lifts from the bottom just like a real insect. You can control the speed by making your mends more or less extreme until you find a consistent speed that works. Even though stone-flies crawl to the banks when they emerge, there are so many here that the fish take them out of the current frequently. More important, though, is the motion of the fly coming to the sur-face. Fish absolutely cannot resist the instinct to chase.'

"Martin had heard enough and began to cast again, even before Woodsy had finished talking. This time my grandfather choked up on the rod, putting his fingers against the cane as well as the cork. The fly sank and then swung, and a fish struck immediately. Martin lifted quickly but much more gently this time, and the fish was on. Martin stood up and yelled. He yelled louder every time the fish jumped, and he yelled when he finally got him to the net."

Jerry can see that Bobby is beginning to nod off, so he stokes the fire in the woodstove and then slams its heavy door shut. Bobby is startled awake by the loud clang of the door. Jerry pours him some more coffee and says, "Stay with me, Bobby, because I don't think these two hounds can understand any of this."

Bobby sits up a little in his chair. "Yes, I'm with you. Martin is on a rock yelling. Your grandfather reminds me of me, but go on."

Jerry continues. "Over the years, Martin and Woodsy became the best of friends and fished all over the county together, perfecting the act of imitating emerging insects. Between them their fly-tying capabilities were unmatched in the local area. As other anglers clung to the classic wet flies, Martin and Woodsy had met the fish at the level of the insect, and it was a huge advantage in almost all of the local Oregon waters.

"The friends learned plenty about trout together over the years, but eventually Woodsy's family moved farther into the woods, and Martin was left to ply the rivers on his own. Martin grew, and life stayed generally the same. He would go to school, do his chores, and fish. His weekends were dedicated to fishing. Sometimes he would go all the way to the coast to fish, or even to the eastern deserts of Oregon. Then one day something incredible happened.

"On a bright Saturday morning in August 1921 my grandfather arrived at his favorite run on his favorite river. Standing right in Martin's favorite spot was a tall thin man who was sporting knickers, a creel, and a fancy shirt and jacket that all matched. Now, my grandfather was a little upset to have to share his spot with someone other than his old friend Woodsy, so he approached the stranger slowly and asked him his name.

"Apparently, the stranger wasn't the least bit startled, and in a heavy English accent he said, 'My name is Sir Alfred Thames. I am from London, England, and am considered the greatest angler of the fly to ever grace my land and certainly yours. Now, if you don't mind, peasant boy, I am about to educate your American trout.'

"Needless to say, my grandfather was stunned. The guy looked just like his picture."

Suddenly Bobby was wide-awake. "Do you mean to tell me that this English angler just happened to show up in Podunk Oregon sometime during the early nineteen hundreds and happened to be fishing alone on your grandfather's favorite river? Well, let the fairy tale continue."

Jerry frowns and says, "Look, you don't have to believe it, but apparently this Sir Alfred Thames was headed down to San Francisco for a big convention and casting tournament at Golden Gate Park. He just happened to get off a boat in Portland and had a few days to kill before his next boat headed down the coast. Somehow he made it into the countryside and ended up on my grandfather's stream."

"Okay, okay, I believe you. Sorry for the interruption," Bobby says with as much sincerity as he can muster at this late hour. "I'll let you finish so I can get some sleep."

Jerry continues, "Now, you have to understand—Martin was young, but he was a very accomplished angler, and, after all, these were his home waters. So that coupled with youthful pride was all it took for Martin to challenge Sir Alfred Thames to an afternoon fishing derby.

"Sir Alfred Thames laughed at the boy's request but agreed, thinking it would help pass the time and was better than fishing alone anyhow. Martin set the simple rules: Whoever could release the most fish before the shadows were completely on the river won. The only other rule was that the anglers had to stay in sight of one another. It was agreed by both that they would work their way downstream for the afternoon. The loser was to never fish this body of water again, and the winner, well, the winner won. Just like that the derby was on.

"Sir Alfred Thames had no idea what he had gotten himself into. He grabbed his wet flies and tied on his all-time favorite, the Queen's Iron Blue Fancy. It was a good-size wet fly. Thames looked, but he couldn't see what Martin had tied on.

"Martin had reached carefully into that black wood fly box and grabbed his best stonefly imitation. He saw that the river had little to no activity, and he knew that these fish would go crazy on stonefly nymphs in the coming weeks, so by now they must have seen many naturals bouncing along the river bottom.

"There isn't much left of the story to tell. Martin spent most of the afternoon letting the Brit go first through the runs. Martin stayed just close enough so that most of the fish he caught would run and jump right behind where Sir Alfred Thames stood. It was no contest. Thames caught one or two fish per run, and Martin caught no less than a half dozen. Thames spent his time mending downstream and swinging his wet fly, attracting the occasional hardy trout, while Martin spent the day mending upstream, creeping his fly in front of fish and then raising it promptly off the bottom, playing on the trout's most primordial urge to strike.

"When the day was over, the two anglers walked back toward town together. Sir Alfred was visibly shaken by the drubbing he had taken from a fourteen-year-old, but he was also mesmerized by the young boy's skill. In the two hours it took to walk to town, the anglers swapped fishing tales and became fast friends. Sir Alfred gave my grandfather a fine split-cane rod for winning the contest, which my grandfather had buried with him when he died. He did this so he would be able to fish in heaven, he said. The end."

Bobby yawns deeply and rises from his chair. "Jerry, thank you very much for tonight's tale. I learned two very important things. First, you want me to try a swinging-fly technique when the river's completely void of activity. Second, don't give all your fly rods away when you're finally too old to fish, because if you don't have your gear in heaven, you're screwed. I imagine that the streams there must be pretty darn good. Now, if you will excuse me, I'm headed for the couch. By the way, why didn't your grandfather have his fly box buried with him, too?"

"He actually was buried with his fly-tying kit. He figured that the insects are surely different up there."

Jerry goes to his room, and Bobby lies down on the couch. Skeets and Milo stay in front of the woodstove. The men and the hounds are asleep in minutes. The snow piles up until dawn, then finally, just before daybreak, the clouds loosen their hold on the mountains, and the morning sky gives the words *royal blue* new meaning.

CHAPTER 8

FISHING THE MIDGE

Both anglers awake to the sound of the hounds, crying to be let outside. The sky is bright blue, and the world outside the farmhouse is pillow white. The reflection of the sun off the snow is so bright that it hurts to look directly out the window without sunglasses. While Jerry makes breakfast, Bobby works at cutting the fingers off a pair of wool gloves for the day's fishing. He is also having a good time teasing Jerry about being stuck in the cellar, and how he, Bobby, who was most recently deemed the best fly angler in the valley, had to save him.

Jerry takes this abuse in good form, and by the time the friends arrive at the river, he has vowed never to build a lodgepole ladder again. The air is brisk, and a steady breeze encourages Bobby and Jerry to put their gloves on immediately. Due to the cool temperatures and bright sun, Jerry doubts that they will see any kind of surface activity today. They grab their gear and start to break trail through the snow to reach Fairsized Creek, the hounds running beside them.

Jerry couldn't have been more wrong about the insect activity. There are midges everywhere—so many, in fact, that the snowy banks look as if someone had waded upstream with a pepper grinder. It is high noon, and there are heads everywhere:

Trout after trout gorge on the surface. The silvery glare on the water's surface makes each rise dimpled and pronounced, accentuating the numbers of rising fish.

Bobby looks at Jerry and says, "Jerry, if all these fish in this run are going at it like this, then most likely that big rainbow upriver is doing the same thing. I'm going up there to find out."

Jerry replies, "He probably is, and you probably should, but I'm starting right here, so have fun."

TERRANCE IS indeed upriver, gluttonously eating on the surface. Midges skate around everywhere. For Terrance, looking up through the surface glare is like a person watching the fuzz on a broken TV. This doesn't deter Terrance from eating, though. He focuses on the midges that are clustered in large groups, mating on the water's surface. He is also free to eat the hundreds of crippled and stillborn midges that come by singly. Terrance isn't being fussy; he simply eats whatever will hold still long enough to be an easy meal. This is the first time in a month that this many bugs are hatching at once, and Terrance eats with reckless abandon. The cold water temperature is the only reason Terrance won't stray too far from his lane. Energy conservation is a concern, but for now moving around isn't necessary. Terrance simply sits and tilts up and down on the outside edge of a slow back eddy.

BEFORE HE leaves, Bobby smiles and asks, "Hey, Jerry, before I go, any hints on fishing the midge?"

"The first things to keep in mind when fishing the midge are to have good patterns, a good eye, and, the most important thing, have a trailing shuck on your fly. I also like to fish midge patterns in tandem as dries, with the more visible one up front," Jerry says.

"You should also keep in mind that just because the glare on the water is bad this time of year doesn't mean the fish can't see you. Anglers tend to think that if it's hard to see the fish, it's just as hard for the fish to see them. This is sometimes true, but not always. I have watched plenty of anglers blow it during midge hatches because they weren't willing to stalk the fish. Maybe they didn't want to crawl and kneel in the snow or were just fooled by the glare, got too close in an upright position, and scared the fish. Regardless of why the fish were scared, none of these anglers kept a low profile.

"When you see that fish, Bobby, stay low and go slowly. You want to be close enough to see that your flies are in the surface film but not so close that you spook the fish."

Bobby searches his fly box for a proper midge pattern with a trailing shuck. He finds a few flies tied by Rene Harrop with CDC and tiny grizzly hackle tips for trailing shucks. He shows these to Jerry, which is a mistake, because he ends up forking over a few of these nice patterns to his friend the fishing guide. In trade he asks Jerry for a little more insight on the trailing shuck.

Jerry begins, "Well, the reason why a trailing shuck is used on a midge fly pattern is the same as why a Sparkle Dun is fished during a baetis hatch. It is also along the same lines as fishing a cripple. The fly just looks like an easier meal to the fish. The fish know that they will expend fewer calories by grabbing the easiest meal. In the winter, this simple act is practiced to an extreme by the trout.

"When anglers buy fly patterns with trailing shucks, it also becomes important to know how to dress the fly. Even on a size 18 dry fly, if there is a shuck I will take the time to dress the body of the fly with a liquid or waxy floatant so the fly is buoyant for a good amount of time and leaves a nice impression in the surface film. I will then dress the wing and hackle with the brush applicator in my dry-shake floatant so I have good visibility of at least part of my fly, and then finally I will put my own saliva on the trailing shuck so that the fish can see part of the fly stuck in the water. This is all to make sure that the fly serves the purpose that it was tied for. The fly is visible to the fish as well as to me, and the shuck is in the surface film so the fish can see an easy opportunity.

"Now, when you get upriver, take a midge cluster pattern, like a Griffith's Gnat, and use its dark body as a silhouette against the glare. Behind it you can put a trailing shuck pattern, like your Harrop fly there, and tie it to the hook shank of the gnat with about fifteen inches of tippet. Now you have a fly—the gnat—that you can see, and a very effective fish catcher—the trailing shuck midge."

Bobby listens intently to everything Jerry says, but he can't shake the eagerness and excitement that is building with every word and every rising fish he can see in the riffle. He searches his fly boxes and finds a nice Griffith's Gnat that will serve as his lead fly and indicator. About the time Bobby is rigged and ready, Jerry finally stops talking, says good luck, and heads for the water.

Bobby heads upstream with one big fish on his mind. He hasn't fished to the big 'bow since he stung him with the hook a few months ago. As Bobby walks briskly through the streamside

snow, he thinks about all that has happened and about every-thing that he's learned since he met Jerry. It occurs to him that this big fish had become a bit of an angling obsession for him. This fish has been a part of his life as long as his new friend Jerry has. He arrives at the big trout's run, stops, and then says aloud to no one in particular, "Maybe I have two friends in this valley; I just haven't met this one face to face yet."

He walks to the water's edge and searches the small back eddy on the far side of the creek. It isn't long before he sees the big trout rising. The only problem he can see, other than the short drift he knows he is going to get, is the fact that there are at least twelve other trout also nosing up to midges in the same eddy.

TERRANCE THE trout has been urgently feeding throughout a great portion of the hatch. The midge hatch has progressed far enough that many clusters formed in the eddy where the tiny insects could find each other most easily. The circling effect of the currents essentially rounds the insects up. The midges pile into clusters on the water in order to procreate, and many have already done so and are dead or dying in the back eddy. For Terrance, there are many opportunities to eat. There are still midges hatching, there are clusters, and there are spent bugs swirling endlessly above him. The eddy is essentially blanketed with midges. Many of the fish that previously were out feeding in the current are now swimming into the back eddy to eat on the smorgasbord.

All the fish had seen big hatches of these chironomids before and know that the swirling currents fill with food as the hatch activity strengthens. The competition is kept to a minimum, with the occasional fish chasing another to claim space, but in general there is so much food that the fish mostly concentrate on eating. Of course, none of these fish would try to chase Terrance—he is by far the biggest and strongest fish in the run—and as the fish swim in slow circles around the eddying current and eat, they all stay out of his way.

BOBBY UNDERSTANDS that he has a chance to catch the big 'bow in the far eddy, but he also knows it will be a bit of a crap shoot to get the fly in front of one particular fish among all the noses repeatedly poking up through the surface film.

He wades out very slowly, much more slowly than he had approached in the summer. He does this for two reasons: He doesn't want to spook the fish during the low waters of winter, and he wants to be physically closer to the fish and the eddy than usual. The closer he gets, the better drift he knows he will get, as well as a better view of his flies on the water.

Once Bobby gets close enough he crouches. He is able to put one of his knees down on a nice flat cobble on the stream bottom. He'll fish from this low-profile position—a lesson Jerry has constantly reinforced—as long as his legs will let him. He strips very little line off his reel and flips out a short cast into the near edge of the eddy. He makes a quick upstream mend with a flick of his wrist and sets the Griffith's Gnat in the back eddy. Once he sees it silhouetted against the glare on the water, he is able to look behind it and find the smaller fly he had tagged onto it.

Almost instantly, Bobby sees a nose appear a few inches to the left of the back fly. He is mesmerized at the sight of a nice-size

fish, which tilts confidently up and smacks down on the Griffith's Gnat. It seems like an eternity to Bobby before his brain
recognizes what is happening and sends the message to his
hands to do something about it.

Bobby sets the hook gently, and the fish is on. It isn't the big
head he had hoped to see, but that is a matter for later. Right now
there is seventeen inches of rainbow leaping straight up from the
middle of the creek like a performing dolphin at Sea World.
Bobby has the fish hooked on 6X and knows he'll have to back
out of the current to land this trout. He keeps his profile low as
he heads back to the bank he had started on. Once on the bank
he is able to walk toward the fish, gain some line, and pull the fish
out of the current into some soft water near the gravel.

Gently holding the fish in the water to revive it, Bobby can't
believe how much his hands hurt. Bobby is used to doing this
during the warmer months, so he didn't expect it, and Jerry had
neglected to warn him. At about the same time he can no longer
endure the cold water, the fish finally shakes to life and hurriedly
swims off.

Bobby rises, breathes into his cupped freezing hands, and
looks back across the river to the eddy. The fish are still in there
rising like nothing had happened, including the big one. Bobby
slowly works his way out to the same spot as before and kneels
on the same flat cobble on the creek bottom.

He can see the big 'bow circling the eddy, tilting up to a
midge about every four to five seconds. Bobby casts, and again
he watches his flies settle into the eddy with the thousands of
other naturals. He makes a quick upstream mend and concentrates on the back fly with the trailing shuck. He sees the big fish

turn in the direction of his fly. He quickly glances to see how much time he has left in his drift before the current yanks his line from the eddy, then looks back at the fish. It is close. The line slowly starts to bow downriver. Bobby lifts the rod tip high, trying to buy precious time as the fish nears.

The huge trout tilts once, swims forward, tilts again on another midge cluster, and swims forward a bit more. Suddenly he is right in front of Bobby's rear fly. By now the current had bowed Bobby's line downriver and is beginning to pull the leader straight. Bobby has about two seconds of drift left as the big 'bow tilts up on his fly, ready to eat it. Then the fly is gone, and Bobby, excited, reacts instantly, gently setting the hook.

It only takes Bobby a few seconds to realize what has just happened as he sees a fourteen-inch fish leap on the end of his line. Just before the current could pull the line from the eddy altogether, the smaller fish had grabbed the Griffith's Gnat before the big rainbow could close his mouth on Bobby's trailing shuck pattern. His heart sinks a bit, but he is also able to breathe again. He quickly lands the fish and returns to the eddy, but the big one is gone. There are still a few nice fish rising, but Bobby missed today's chance to land the trophy of this run.

Bobby waits twenty minutes for the fish to rise again, but it doesn't. He decides to explore upriver a bit before heading back to find Jerry. He fishes on up and does fine, although he can't seem to shake a light feeling of the blues, having again come up short on a fish he isn't sure he will have too many more opportunities to catch.

CHAPTER 9

FISHING AND MATH

Bobby finds Jerry back at the truck a few hours after they had originally split. Jerry is fast asleep in the bed of the pickup. Skeets and Milo, who are also asleep, are using him as a pillow. Bobby sets his rod on the hood of the truck and takes his waders off. By the time he packs away his gear and is ready to go, his friend is beginning to stir to life.

Jerry sits up, rubs his eyes, and inquires, "Well, Bobby, did you get him?"

Bobby shakes his head and says, "No, I didn't, but I was really close. Had it not been for my success with the rest of the general trout population I may have had a chance, because he was there and he was feeding."

"Well, what can you do but try again?" Jerry says.

Bobby isn't quite in the mood to hear any clichés and doesn't reply. It is a quiet ride, despite the great afternoon of fishing the two friends had just had. The biggest rainbow in Fairsized Creek had both men on the hook and was playing them, even as they left the water.

When Jerry reaches the main road of the valley, he turns right, in the opposite direction of his farmhouse, and heads toward town.

"Where are we going?" Bobby asks.

Jerry grins and whistles for a second, acting like he won't answer, and then responds, "How does a steak smothered in blue cheese and a pint of the darkest, driest pilsner we can find sound?"

"How soon until we get there?"

Fifteen minutes later the two friends find themselves in the comfy confines of Stuva's Grill, with Mr. Stuva himself bringing them pints of beer and plates of rich, western overindulgence. They eat and talk casually about growing up, ex-girlfriends, and the best music to get over a broken heart. Bobby prefers straightforward rock 'n' roll, like the Stones or the Doors, while Jerry leans more toward the merits of jazz, such as Jimmy Smith or Miles Davis, to repair the heart and soul.

An hour after sitting down in Stuva's Grill and being treated like the two most important people alive, both anglers' moods and energy levels had considerably brightened. The Hayden berry cobbler placed in front of them, piping hot and served over a deep bed of vanilla ice cream, only heightens this.

Bobby says, "If the river we just left isn't Nirvana, Jerry, then this place surely must be."

"The two of them combined are most likely a close second," Jerry replies.

After dinner they sip spiked cider while relaxing in front of the fireplace that Mr. Stuva keeps burning hot into the wee hours of the night. They sit and talk about life in general, and then, more specifically, about the day's events.

Jerry has spent many an evening in front of this fireplace sipping cider. For Bobby, who is used to the hustle and bustle of city restaurants, it is a special treat to be able to linger.

About the time their second round of cider is being served, Bobby returns to his usual inquisitive self and asks, "What is it, in a nutshell, that makes you as great a trout angler as you obviously are? What is the one thing that is most important to you as a fly angler?"

This gives Jerry pause and even makes him blush, but only for a moment. Then he answers, "Fly fishing and math," and takes a sip of his cider.

Bobby knows right away that he is now going to have to ask Jerry to explain himself and that the answer is most likely going to be a long one. He decides he'd better pace himself on the cider. Then he asks Jerry to explain.

"Bobby," said Jerry, "you are opening the door to a soliloquy that would make Shakespeare proud."

There is no response from Bobby, who sinks deeper into his chair. So Jerry begins.

"Fishing and math is just a way of saying that catching a trout on a fly is simply a matter of recognizing how the fish reacts in its environment, in relation to your fly as well as to real insects. This, in turn, is influenced by things such as insect activity, fly size, fly appearance, water depth, current speed, barometric pressure, fishing pressure, and, finally, angler skill.

"Insect activity comes into play when deciding what fly to fish, but it is even more important when determining where to fish. When insect activity is strong, what most commonly happens is that fish will move to shallow water. The reason for this is in the math.

"A fish wants to live in a safe place. This usually means near structure, in deep water, or, ideally, both. What happens then is a

trout will establish feeding areas dependent on the available food source. In other words, fish may move to different locations near their safe spot in order to feed on different kinds of prey.

"The fish now has a holding area as well as one or more feeding areas. This is not to say a trout won't feed opportunistically in his safe spot when given a good chance.

"During a hatch or spinner fall of any decent size, the surface of the water, as well as the depths in any particular run on a river, will begin to fill with insects. Now, if a fish were to remain in deeper water, let's say on the bottom of a six-foot hole in the run, near its safe spot, the amount of insects in the stratos of water will be spread out. Let's say there are twenty nymphs, available all at once. The fish is only going to expend a certain amount of calories to ingest this food. The food must represent more calories to the fish than the calories the fish would expend to get the food. Every day that you fish, the first thing to consider if you can't see fish actively feeding is how much energy the fish are going to be willing to expend in order to eat.

"Now during the same hatch, in the same run, at the same moment, let's say there are twenty available nymphs entering the shallow riffle at the head of the run. The same fish can now swim up to the shallows, move a very short distance, and expend very little energy to ingest the same calories that he would have had to swim farther and burn many more calories for in the deeper water.

"So the first thing you should do when you approach the water is take a careful inventory of what is happening in and on the water. Whether you can see fish feeding is your first clue to how much energy the fish will expend, and you can choose your fly accordingly. A certain size fly or a certain movement may be necessary to draw strikes. I'm not saying to always go to a big fly or a subsurface fly when the fish aren't rising because the choice is relative to many other factors, such as weather, subsurface activity, geographic region, time of day, and so on. A big fly in the fall may not be a big fly in the spring. A big fly on Fairsized Creek is a small fly in Well-Known River. Learn the water by putting the time in, and then these judgments will become easy to make when it's time to choose a fly.

"The other way to find the fish is to start casting and fish the whole run from top to bottom. In any case, the result will be the same, and the same conclusions will be deduced. Stopping to take inventory, either by sight, by sample, or both, is a way to increase your time spent over the most productive waters and increase your catch rate."

Jerry stops for a moment and takes a pull from his cider. Bobby nods at him to go on, showing no signs of falling asleep like the last time Jerry was long-winded. After all, this is Jerry's fishing philosophy that he seems to be pouring forth, and Bobby doesn't want to do anything to discourage Jerry from telling him about it.

Jerry leans back and continues, "Let's go a bit further now in locating the fish. What time of year is it? What's the temperature? What time of day is it? These are just a few things to think about when trying to decide what insect is predominately hatching or spinning at any given instance. The next step is to understand the habits of the insects: where they collect as spinners and from what part of the river they hatch.

"For instance, a stonefly crawls to the banks as a nymph and loves overhanging foliage as a spinner. So when I fish a stonefly nymph I consider where the real nymphs are and what they are doing. This goes for all other insects as well. A drake may emerge from the mud and gravel in the middle of a run in the river but may spin over the fast riffles upstream from these areas, so during a hatch the fish work the middle and back of the run, and during the spinner fall they work the busy waters at the head of the run. Simply put, what insect is available, what it is doing, and where it is doing it come to the forefront. Do you remember how the midges collected heaviest in the back eddy today?"

Bobby is surprised by the sudden question and nods.

"That is exactly what I'm talking about here. By concentrating your time over the most bugs and the most fish, and knowing that the eddy was the place to look during heavy midge activity, put you right in the game. Simply knowing what insect was hatching was all you needed to know in order to determine where the bugs would be before you got there. The math was in the knowledge that the fish would gather where the insects concentrated, and being aware of the nature of the insect is what gave you a big advantage. You could spend more time fishing and less time locating fish.

"I've gotten a bit off track talking about locating fish, so let's get back to the math of fish and energy. When we talk about a fish that will only move so far to ingest an insect, based on how much energy the insect or insects represent, we then begin to get into fly choice. When choosing a fly, the two most important factors are its size and appearance.

"Let's say a trout is hanging out near his safe spot, not actively feeding. We can get the fish to move to the fly if it is a rough representation of something in the trout's immediate diet and is acting as such, but only if the distance between the fly and the fish is on par with how willing the fish is to expend the energy to consume the fly. This can also be influenced by several factors, such as how cold the water is. The fish will obviously be more active during prime months when water temperatures are more ideal rather than during more stressful times of the season. These months may vary from river to river and region to region, but the fact remains that a fish's activity is hugely influenced by water temperature.

"How far a fish will move is also determined by the current speed. If the fish is near fast water, he may have to dart out and then swim hard to regain a position in softer water. In slower water it becomes more a question of how far a fish must go to cross a hole or pool, and how this will leave the fish more vulnerable to predators in the process of burning the calories to capture the prey.

"Fish movement is also influenced by high or low barometric pressure. Barometric change may set the fish on the bottom due to a lack of insect activity, whereas a consistent ceiling of high or low pressure may spark loads of insect activity. These occurrences may change several times a week during the winter or several times a day during the spring. It is the angler's job to get in tune with the surroundings in order to deduce what is necessary to encourage a trout to strike, be it a certain fly, a certain movement of a fly, or both."

Jerry is talking faster than ever, and Bobby can almost see his friend's mind churning with the elements of calories, distance, barometric pressure, and temperature. Bobby doesn't want to interrupt and slow him down.

Jerry continues, "While we're on the subject of pressure, take into consideration the fishing pressure on a given body of water. This will also influence the fish and how they feed. It will, at the very least, give you some idea of how tactfully and suavely you need to approach the water. In other words, fishing pressure will help you discern whether you are on a casual upstream fishing trek or if you're on your knees for hours at a time over one pool.

"Now, back to fly size and its appearance. The size of the fly is somewhat determined by the location of the fish and, of course, what the available food sources are at the moment. In the case of a fish holding near its safe spot, the fly most likely needs to draw the fish's attention in such a way that it can't be refused. This is where anglers who are well versed and practiced in the arts of streamer fishing and swinging nymphs will excel, because large representations of certain prey can get the fish to strike on instinct as much as out of hunger. The way the fly looks isn't the most important thing. In this case a large fly representing a big meal that is fished in a convincing way may be all that is necessary to get the fish to chase and strike. The other approach to catching the same sedentary fish is to hit the trout right on the nose with a smaller pattern, but this usually means knowing exactly where the fish is sitting, or mining a huge area with a strike indicator set-up.

"The dry-fly analogy of this situation is simply whether your fly is big enough that the fish is willing to risk being seen by predators and expend the energy to get to it, even though it may fly off. This is where cripples and emergers enter the math game, but we'll get to that in a minute.

"Let's quickly touch on fly appearance. This becomes more important in a hatch situation, when the fish are most likely in shallow water. A fish that is sitting shallow is there for a reason, and that is usually to eat, with the exception of the spawn. Fish that are sitting shallow are the easiest target for the fly angler because the fish are there to eat and are generally aggressive. Not catching fish in shallow-water situations is most often due to angler error rather than fish not being on the bite. This error is usually from being seen or heard by the fish. Both are easy to remedy: by taking the time to be stealthy and by having the proper leader set-ups so that the line doesn't spook the fish.

"Let's say we are fishing in a shallow riffle, and the trout are locked on eating pink Albert emergers one after another. Suddenly, fly choice becomes important in order to catch the same fish that hours ago would have eaten any well-presented streamer pattern in the depths of the pool. Now there is such a multitude of Alberts emerging in the twelve inches of water that the fish are sitting in, the fishes' instincts have gone into overdrive. They know that the safest thing to do is to eat as much of this easy prey as they can. At a moment like this, putting on standard patterns like Hare's Ears or Prince Nymphs, no matter how well tied or presented, can be fruitless. The passing angler might catch an occasional fish, but the in-tune angler is going to excel at this moment by placing well-tied Pink Albert Emergers into the fray.

"The big picture here, Bobby, is to use what you know about the fish in a certain body of water. Think about what the fishes' concerns are at any given moment, keeping in mind that fish are opportunistic and gluttonous. Fish have to, and want to, eat.

"Now, before we go any further, I have to see a man about a horse. If you don't mind, I'll take another one of those ciders, and if you're having another, I'll buy this round."

Jerry stands up, stretches a bit, and heads for the rest room. Bobby also stands and stretches, and he goes up to the bar for more cider. A few minutes later the two friends are again well placed in front of the fire, and Jerry picks up where he left off.

"The math in locating fish and choosing a fly is simply to have a basic understanding of what fish will do to eat. It is having an understanding of how fish eat and survive on a minute-to-minute basis. Where will the fish be under certain conditions? And what do they need to see to be provoked into striking? This doesn't mean that you have to take your calculator to the stream or physically weigh the differences of specific nymphs. You just need to keep in mind what the fish are going through to survive, and what their basic nature is when it comes to feeding on different types of prey.

"The rest of what I have to say we have talked about plenty of times during our past fishing days together, but let me just touch on it briefly before we call this a night."

Bobby encourages Jerry to go on, so he does. "Fishing and math can be very important when considering how a fish eats. This normally means a fish will take the easiest prey available. When considering insect activity, a fish will almost always take the easiest insects to capture. I'm sure you've been told and have noticed on your own that often the rattiest-looking flies are the best fish-catchers. But have you ever stopped to wonder why? Most likely the reason is because even the best-tied flies don't look nearly as good as the real thing; therefore, the artificial fly looks like it is that much easier to catch when a fish sees it, as long as it's a rough imitation of what the trout is already eating. So fishing an artificial may be an advantage in its own right, but fishing a ratty-looking fly may make the imitation look all that much easier for the fish to catch.

"Every time we have fished cripples, emergers, and spent-wing patterns, we have been doing it for reasons of math. We are showing fish artificial insects that look like sure things. In other words, the fish is almost guaranteed a meal for the mere effort of rising to it, as opposed to rising on a fully emerged dun that is flapping its wings, bouncing around, and ready to fly off at any second, or an ovipositing insect during a spinner fall that may also be bouncing from place to place.

"Showing a trout a fly that is easy to capture, taking the time to tie the right knots, and dressing the fly properly are some of the things that are very important. However, there is one more basic thing to take into our giant fish-catching equation: angler skill. It is the final step to influencing a trout to eat. After an angler makes a few failed attempts, naturally the fish will get scared and stop eating. Being able to step to the plate, analyze the situation, and make the right choices in a timely manner are all part of the trout-catching equation. What anglers lack in skill, they can make up in patience. No one learns anything by spooking all the fish. At some point anglers need to be willing to step back and observe in order to step forward and produce hook-ups. Anglers' skill isn't judged by how many fish are caught or how big they are so much as how effortlessly they can approach a situation and solve the fish-catching puzzle. Reading a situation and reacting to it efficiently are two of the traits that separate good and great anglers."

Bobby jumps in and stops Jerry for a minute. "Jerry, what do you mean these are two of the things that separate good and great anglers? You obviously think there are other necessary attributes an angler must have to be head and shoulders above the rest, so what else is there?"

Jerry is not ready for this sudden question after Bobby had been sitting quietly for so long, but he had made a leading statement that brought it on, so he tries to answer. "Okay, I just mentioned how an angler's skill is also dependent on the math and ratios I've been talking about for the last twenty minutes. Again, this means, in a nutshell, that the sign of an accomplished angler is not how many fish are caught, but how quickly the angler can approach a situation and produce fish. How many casts will it take? How many fly changes? How much water will be covered? There are many ways to determine one's prowess as an angler should one even want to consider this. Some people don't care how good they are and just want to go fishing, but this casual approach means that these people usually become the best anglers despite themselves.

"To answer your question, Bobby, another thing that separates good and great anglers are line-on-the-water skills, but this is one of many other things. To me, though, it is the single most important attribute that the best of the best have."

"Jerry," Bobby says as he rises from his chair, "I believe you could talk to me until dawn about line-on-the-water skills, but to tell you the truth, right now my mind is so full of numbers, fish, flies, and cider that I don't think I could absorb another word. What do you say we call it a night?"

Jerry is more than ready to swap fishing theory for sleep. The two friends settle their tab with Mr. Stuva and head back to the farmhouse.

CHAPTER 10

LINE-ON-THE-WATER SKILLS
ARE MORE IMPORTANT
THAN CASTING SKILLS

Bobby is the first one awake the next morning. The couch he had slept on apparently had thrown a spring during the night. Although his back is a little rigid, Bobby thinks how much better this is compared to the alternative, a generic motel room. It is cold, so he quickly jumps up and lights a fire in the woodstove and then proceeds to start some coffee brewing. He gets back under his blankets and waits for both to heat up.

About the same time the house is warming and the coffee is steaming, Jerry emerges from his room with a stack of books. He places them on the kitchen table, tells Bobby to look them over, and starts to make breakfast.

Jerry washes up and fries eggs and bacon in a heavy skillet. Bobby pores over the books, examining each one. There are several fly-fishing histories and a book of short stories. There are a few older books as well, describing fly patterns and famous fly tyers. Jerry tells Bobby to pay close attention to the histories of fly fishing.

Over breakfast it is decided that a lazy afternoon of fishing is in order, if for nothing else to at least try and find Bobby's big rainbow. The dishes are quickly washed, dried, and put away, and then both anglers retire to their respective readings for a few more hours while the winter sun slowly warms the valley floor.

Bobby reads random chapters from each of the books, starting with casting tournaments in Golden Gate Park and a chapter about Theodore Gordon and how the Quill Gordon dry fly became popular. In another book he reads all about the famous steelhead rivers in Oregon and about the famous and infamous anglers that fished these waters. There are books with photos of British anglers fishing for tarpon off the Florida coast, in plain view of clipper ships sailing by in the background. It's clear to Bobby that the history of fly fishing is as rich and detailed as any other sport. In many ways it is more significant, due in part to the fact that fishing with flies was a means of survival before it became a sport. This makes it seemingly Olympic in nature: Fly fishing, originating as a survival skill and then becoming a modern game that continues to evolve, with its heroes and mythical figures, seems much like the world of Olympic track and field.

Bobby continues to voraciously read through sections of each book, losing all track of time. If it hadn't been for the strong sunlight beating through the front window, Bobby would have read the day away. Realizing the afternoon heat is at its peak, he shuts the book he is thumbing through and yells to Jerry. A few minutes later Jerry emerges again from his room, obviously roused from an afternoon slumber.

"Did you get a lot of quality reading done this morning, Jerry?" Bobby asks.

Jerry rubs his eyes and heads for his waders, which are draped on a chair near the woodstove.

"As it turns out, I was a few hours short of a full night's sleep, so I needed to get my internal clock back in order. Now, are we going fishing, or would you rather read those books I gave you?"

Bobby chooses fishing and heads outside to warm up the truck. A few minutes later, Jerry and Bobby are off to the banks of Fairsized Creek.

Jerry is quiet during the ride to the river and then breaks his silence. "Bobby, today while you were reading those books, how much stuff did you read about mending a fly line on the water?"

Bobby thinks for a moment and then says, "I don't think I read anything, except for a mention here or there about upstream mends in the steelhead chapters. Why?"

Jerry responds, "How many famous line menders did you read about?"

Bobby shakes his head. "None."

"Do you remember last night while we were leaving the restaurant, we briefly talked about line-on-the-water skills?"

"I remember," Bobby responds.

"Well," Jerry says, "there is plenty in those books about famous casters and fly tyers, and you may have read about fly-fishing trailbreakers and founders of the saltwater game. But my question was loaded. I know that there's nothing in those books about anyone named Jacob Mend, or the Mend River, because there's no such thing.

"My point here, Bobby, is that the best fly anglers are masters of controlling the line on the water. The fly is always working for them. If the fly moves when they are fishing, it is because it's supposed to. If the fly remains drag free after they cast thirty feet upriver and allow it to drift thirty feet down, rest assured they can do it every time.

"One thing all these anglers have in common is that they are constantly aware of what the line is doing and is going to do in the current. Great fly anglers are able to recognize and remedy any drag on the fly before it happens. They do this by constantly making subtle adjustments throughout the drift. This may mean they are feeding line out of the rod tip, or stripping it in, all the while making adjustments and staying ready to strike. When you're fly fishing, Bobby, think about mending as something you always do while the fly is drifting, as opposed to mending once and watching your fly or indicator drift."

This catches Bobby's attention. He looks at Jerry and says, "You have been a regular fountain of fly-fishing information for the last twenty-four hours, haven't you?"

Jerry grumbles something as he rolls down his window. Bobby continues, "So I did all that reading today in order to learn what isn't there?"

Jerry cuts in, "Having excellent line-on-the-water skills in fly fishing is like a silent pause in music. It is where the music comes from: Without the silence, there is no music. When you're fly fishing, you may have all the casting skill in the world, but if you are not taking care of business during the drift, then you're not realizing your fly-fishing potential and are probably catching half the fish you could be. Anglers have to excel at both skills. Mending the line on moving water is the ultimate contact anglers can have with their immediate surroundings."

Bobby is amazed. In a nutshell, casting, as far as Jerry is concerned, is not the essence of the sport—at least not by itself. Jerry is obviously giving equal billing to the art of mending line.

The river is in view, and Jerry pulls the truck off the road, narrowly missing a snowy embankment with his right front fender. The two friends rig their rods and once again are on the banks of Fairsized Creek. They figure that they have about two hours of fishing before it will be too cold and dark. Jerry suggests that they go directly upriver to the back eddy Bobby was in yesterday. They have enough time to see if the big rainbow is active. Bobby agrees, and up the river they go.

IT HAS BEEN a long time since Terrance the trout has been hooked. There have only been a few moments during the fall season that have put him extremely on guard. One moment had been this morning, when an adult otter had discreetly entered his pool. The otter had briefly chased Terrance, but luckily a big white fish, an easier meal for the otter, had come along. The otter eventually caught his lunch and left. However, the otter's scent lingering in the water is a reminder that Terrance always needs to be ready for danger. The other fish in the run that had seen the otter are also wary, and most of them spend a great deal of time sitting very still near the heaviest bottom structure. For the next few hours, when one fish becomes a little spooked, they all do.

The afternoon sun brings slightly warmer water temperatures and another big hatch of midges. There is plenty to eat, but only a few of the trout actively do so. As for Terrance, he needs to fuel his large body, but he is on edge enough to know that he needs to eat very discreetly, regardless of the number of insects on the water's surface. Eating is important, but Terrance isn't going to take any chances.

As the light begins to leave the water in the late afternoon, Terrance slowly slips into the back eddy on the river's edge. He goes all the way to the steep bank and turns downriver in order to face into the eddy's reverse current. Once he is there he sits near the bottom, not moving, and watches. Eventually he is satisfied that the coast is clear, and he slowly rises toward the surface, eating infrequently. He sips in the first midge cluster in his vicinity that he sees and then submerges again until another good-size cluster comes his way. He takes this one as well. Terrance proceeds to eat, but cautiously, never giving in to his gluttonous instinct. The instinct to survive is stronger. Even though the otter had been gone for quite a while, Terrance's focus on survival is going to remain strong all day.

IT TAKES Bobby and Jerry several minutes to locate any rising fish in the big rainbow's run. The rises are so infrequent and spread around that neither angler can be sure if any of the noses he sees is the big 'bow. The sun is no longer on the water in this spot, and the late-afternoon chill had begun. The anglers silently watch, occasionally breathing into a gloved hand to keep their fingers warm.

"I don't see him, Jerry," Bobby finally says.

Jerry replies, "He could be any of those fish or none of them. None of them have risen enough for us to be able to really grasp their size. The strange thing is that there are a lot of bugs on the water, but the fish aren't interested in eating them."

They stare a while longer, and then Bobby speaks up again. "Jerry, since that big fish is nowhere to be seen, why don't we use this time for a clinic on mending? It is obviously very important, and I can say with certainty that I've never thought that much about it or had anyone good show me what I should be doing."

Jerry knows where this is headed and doesn't like the idea of being on stage very much. He considers it for a moment and then realizes that he and Bobby had assumed a sort of teacher-pupil relationship from the beginning. Jerry had brought this upon himself, so why not continue with it? He looks at Bobby and says, "Pick a fish."

This certainly catches Bobby by surprise. Jerry, normally reserved and modest, is going to reveal his confident and highly skilled angling side, which is always there but not always seen. Bobby is excited. Jerry had basically told him that he would catch any target selected, but not in so many words.

Bobby scans the water again, trying to determine which of the inconsistently rising fish he would ignore if he were fishing. Then he spots a small dimple of a rise in the very back side of the eddy. The fish would have to be facing downstream to feed in that spot. In order to catch this fish, Jerry will have to get a drift over three very strong current lanes, a task that even the most experienced fly angler would find difficult.

He points the fish out to Jerry with a sheepish grin, thinking this choice might surprise his friend. Jerry waits a moment until he sees the dimpled rise form that Bobby is pointing at. He waits a few more moments for another rise, and then he wades out toward the fish. Bobby stays by Jerry's left shoulder and wades out with him. He doesn't want to miss a thing.

By now, the late-afternoon glare on the water is incredibly bad, which will only make this harder. Jerry will have to cast a fair distance directly across the stream, locate his fly on the silvery surface, and then work his line in such a way that the fly can grab the upstream current on the eddy's far side. Then, if he is lucky enough—or good enough, in this case—to get the fish to rise to the fly, he'll have to pick up whatever amount of line is laid out over the three current lines in order to set the hook. Bobby thinks that he's chosen well. The closer they get to the eddy, the more confident Bobby becomes that this fish cannot be caught. It would be one thing if the fish was acting gluttonous and eating everything in its lane, but this fish was far from aggressive.

Jerry strips out his line. To be certain, he measures out more length than he needs to reach the other side. Jerry feels that this fish will not give him many chances; it just seems too timid a rise form among all this insect activity.

Jerry is ready to cast. He has tied a single trailing shuck midge pattern onto a twelve-foot, 6X leader. He has dressed the fly to ride high for visibility, but he's made sure that the shuck—made of Z-lon—on this midge pattern is wet and will sink slightly.

Bobby waits in anticipation. He knows Jerry won't cast until the fish has shown some sort of rhythm. This could take a while. He sees the fish rise and notes that even though the rise form is a dimple, the fish probably has some size to it. Neither angler thinks for a moment that this is the big rainbow that Bobby has tried so hard to catch, but it is.

TERRANCE IS feeling as on edge as ever due to a series of small waves that go over his head. The water temperature is beginning to cool, and the midge activity, although strong, is beginning to taper off. Terrance's urge to eat is subsiding, but the fading light and still-plentiful insects make it just tempting enough to keep him in position a few minutes more. Terrance rises infrequently, only eating the most accessible midges.

He rises to a small cluster of midges that are struggling in the cold air. A minute later he rises to a single midge that seems to be stillborn, half in and half out of its shuck.

JERRY HAS seen enough. The fish had just taken a midge cluster off the surface by sipping from underneath. It was as discreet a rise as Jerry had ever seen, but it was there. One second there was a single midge cluster, and then it was gone. Only a few small concentric rings of water remain, but the movement of the silvery surface in the evening glare is enough proof that a fish is there. Jerry waits a moment longer and then begins to false cast.

His line goes out perfectly, seemingly downstream of the fish, but heads with the fly into an upstream eddy current. Jerry holds the rod high, overshoots his target, and then pulls the line and rod slightly back toward him while reach casting across his body. The line and fly land on the water just below the fish. Jerry holds the rod tip high as he throws small loops of line upstream toward the fly. As Jerry does this, the closest main current pulls the back of the line, and in order to fix this he takes a bigger line mend, up into the head of the eddy. He then makes smaller loops upstream to release the fly from any line tension as the fly is sucked up into the eddying current.

Due to the big mend, the fly pulls slightly toward the middle of the eddy and away from the far bank. Jerry realizes that this is bound to happen every time, so now the length of his drift is going to be shorter than he had first guessed. He reaches his arm and upper body forward to get the last few inches of dead drift, then straightens and lightly pulls the line and fly from the eddy.

The fish hadn't risen, and both friends agree that the fly had probably been too far inside of the fish by the time it had drifted up the eddy to the spot of the last rise form. Jerry takes a breath and knows that this presentation will have to be closer to the target. He slowly false casts once and then twice, and then makes the same reach cast he had just performed. Only this time Jerry puts the fly about eight inches from the spot he thinks the last dimple had come from. At about the same moment Jerry is flipping his first loop of line up toward the fly, he sees the dimple again. On instinct, Jerry lifts the rod quickly. In the process he startles Bobby, and both anglers stumble to the fill zones of their waders.

The rod arcs forward, and the line tears quickly from the eddy toward the main current the anglers are standing in. Once the fish catches the current, it turns sideways and begins to move across this current toward the bank that Jerry and Bobby had started from, heading downstream in the process. Jerry leans the rod in the other direction to turn the fish back toward the eddy, but the fish is already turned and heading that way. Jerry has the fish on the reel, and the drag sings. It's at this point that Jerry realizes what is happening. This is no ordinary fish; this is a huge rainbow. It's Bobby's fish!

The fish picks up speed as it tears back across the river. Bobby hollers in excitement, knowing it's a nice fish but not realizing that it's the big 'bow. The line makes a tearing sound as the fly line has trouble keeping up with the magnificent rainbow. Jerry had felt fish do this before and knows what is about to happen: The fish is going to jump. Jerry knows that once it does, Bobby will realize which fish this is and encourage—if not demand—that Jerry do everything possible to land the brute.

Without a moment of hesitation, Jerry picks up his downstream foot. This situates his stance in a sideways pivot, and now he faces back toward the eddy rather than facing downstream. Bobby, who had been standing at Jerry's left shoulder, is momentarily behind him. For the split second Jerry has his back to Bobby, he squeezes the line quickly against the cork. With the pressure of the main current and the speed of the fish, this slight touch on the line is more than enough to pull the hook.

The rod springs out of its arc, and the line hangs limp on the water. The big rainbow is gone. While the trout was bigger than any fish Jerry had caught in two seasons, he knows this isn't his fish to catch. Bobby had put too much time and effort into catching that fish. Bobby had come a long way over the course of the season and was becoming an exceptional angler in many ways; however, he personally saw this big 'bow as his graduation into the ranks of accomplished fly anglers. Jerry figures that until Bobby catches this fish, the two of them will always have a student-teacher relationship, and, for Jerry, fishing goes deeper than this. He wants Bobby to be able to move to the next level, where the act of going fishing takes precedence over the act of catching fish. Jerry loves nothing more than catching big fish, but he is not going to catch a fish that had come to represent so much to his friend.

Bobby is astounded by what he had just witnessed. His first thoughts are only about the take and presentation. He can't believe Jerry's prowess with a fly rod. So what that he had lost such a nice fish? The excitement of the take was what each had anticipated so much and had been accomplished so deftly by Jerry.

As the anglers head back to the bank, Jerry comments on how powerful a sixteen-inch fish that was. He tells Bobby that he figures it was sixteen inches based on the weight of the fish when he first set the hook. He agrees with Bobby that the fish had acted possessed and was obviously strong, but he doesn't seem very disappointed over losing the fish. This makes Bobby suspect that the fish probably wasn't as big as it seemed. To get off the subject, Jerry talks about mending.

"The point I've been trying to make today hasn't been so much about how to mend your line as much as just being aware of it. How you mend your line on the water is always going to be dictated by the currents in any particular spot. I just wanted to stress how important it is to practice mending with as much determination as you would when casting or tying flies. Any decent angler could have cast to the back of that eddy, but not many people know what to do once the fly is there. The only way to learn it is to do it. It is an easy skill to master, but a conscious effort must be made."

For the next hour the friends fish together. They each only catch one fish before it is finally cold and dark enough to drive them off the water. On the way home, Bobby thanks Jerry for a great couple of days of fishing, hospitality, and education. Tomorrow he'll head back to Big City, and he won't be able to return until the middle of the summer. The friends agree to keep in touch for the next few months.

The next morning Jerry takes Bobby to the airport, then goes home and begins to tie flies for the coming season.

CHAPTER 11

WHEN TO FORGET
THE WORDS "LEADER SHY"

I t is a very happy moment when the two friends see each other again. Bobby had been away for a long time, and Jerry had kept busy guiding and tinkering around his small farm. The only significant changes in either of them are Jerry's hair, which had grown longer, and his waistline, which had shed the winter pounds.

Bobby knows from the occasional call or note from Jerry that his big rainbow is still around. If anyone had caught him up until now, they were gracious enough to leave him happy and healthy in his pool.

Today, though, is not going to be spent trying to find this fish. Jerry had arranged for access once again to Grassy Brook. He had offered the landowner some guide days in exchange for access, which had been accepted. He had wanted to fish the trico spinner fall on this water for years, and he thought there would be no better occasion for this than Bobby's visit.

Jerry had picked up Bobby at the airport at the crack of dawn, and they once again head to Grassy Brook in Jerry's old truck. As usual, Jerry's hounds, Skeets and Milo, who keep a lookout for varmints from the bed of the pickup, accompany them. Both men are in high spirits as they spend the ride catching up on the last few months. Jerry had taken two saltwater fishing trips to Mexico and the Bahamas, and Bobby had been promoted twice in his company. Each expresses his happiness about these events to the other. Finally, with one more valley left to cross before Grassy Brook, the topic switches to the local fishing.

Jerry reassures Bobby that he will get a chance to catch his big rainbow tomorrow, but first they need to concentrate on two things: fishing tricos and perhaps some afternoon terrestrial fishing on this trophy stream.

Jerry says as they pull in to the ranch, "The trico spinner fall here is going to be as intense as it is on Fairsized Creek, but the degree of difficulty will be increased by the fact that almost all of Grassy Brook is flat, slow water. This means we need impeccable drifts with fine tippets. Don't be surprised if you see fish following your dry flies from underneath for several feet, trying to decide if they want it."

They emerge from Jerry's truck to almost ninety-degree heat. The air is relatively calm, with an occasional breeze. Over the river they can see enormous clouds of tricos already spinning. As they approach the water, they can see that it is already boiling with pods of fish. They grab their gear and rig up quickly. Bobby is so excited that he is about to jump out of his skin. It has been a long time since he fished, and this special trip is an exciting way to break his dry spell. He thinks about how lucky he is to have a friend in the business, so to speak. He has friends in Big City that give him stock tips, health advice, auto-care opinions, and the like, but none of this information is on par with the perks he gets from his friendship with Jerry.

After covering themselves in sunscreen and mosquito repellent, the two friends head to the stream. They each choose a pod of rising fish and begin to cast, but neither hooks up right away. Both anglers had started with twelve-foot 4X leaders, thinking the lack of angling pressure on this water could mean the fish wouldn't be leader shy, but obviously they are wrong. The best placed casts and drifts are not enough to catch these fish; it is going to take a more discreet approach.

Jerry switches right to 6X, knowing from his past experience on this water that it can sometimes be more demanding than other times, yet there is very little middle ground. He catches fish as soon as he switches. It takes Bobby another fifteen minutes before he hooks up. He had switched to 5X with no luck at all before moving down to 6X. In his mind, though, he knows he has taken the right approach by checking what the fishes' limits are through trial and error. As soon as he switches to 6X, he catches fish repeatedly.

The morning becomes early afternoon, and the spinner fall just keeps coming. Both Jerry and Bobby had caught and released numerous good-size fish, but neither angler is about to walk away until the last trico spinner floats by. Jerry had worked hard at guiding all summer, and Bobby had worked hard at his office in the city for months on end, and they are determined to get their fill.

Some time later, Grassy Brook goes still at last. The insects are gone, and the trout retire to their hiding places under the banks and the overhanging grass. It is 1:00 P.M. when Bobby hears the shout of "Lunch!" just around the bend from where he is finishing up. He reels up and walks the short distance back to the truck.

He finds Jerry sitting on the tailgate. There is an open cooler, and Jerry is already in tears from eating the horseradish on his roast beef sandwich. Bobby sits next to him and swears that lunch had never tasted so good. They compare notes on the morning's fishing. Both men are extremely happy with the trico activity, and both had done extremely well. Bobby finishes up his lunch and asks Jerry what is on tap for the afternoon.

"Well, Bobby, we have access to this water for the whole day, so we may as well try our luck here for a few more hours."

Bobby is more than okay with this idea and excitedly asks, "Should we fish hoppers?"

Jerry responds, "Absolutely. I'm sure other terrestrials like a beetle or ant would work, but a fish hitting a hopper on the surface is one of my favorite sights in the world."

The two friends enjoy their lunch break a while longer and then head back to the stream. They split up after Jerry suggests they do so in order to cover a lot of water. The nature of fishing the grasshopper imitation is for the fish to eat it the first time it sees it or not at all. In order to fish productively it is important to stay on the move. They decide that Jerry will head upstream and work his way down, while Bobby will walk to the opposite end of the pasture and work upstream. They will meet somewhere in the middle, and at that time they'll decide to either keep fishing or head for home, depending on how it is going. They wish one another luck and head off in different directions.

Jerry is completely entranced fifteen minutes later as he watches his huge Dave's Hopper floating down the length of bank opposite him. It brushes against the lowest blades of grass as it drifts. The seconds after this first cast seem like minutes.

Jerry forgets to breathe as he intently watches the fly. He never notices that he is holding his breath, because four feet into the drift, a huge hole opens up in the water under his fly. Jerry has seen this before and half expected this on his first cast. He waits just a moment for the fish to close its mouth on the fly, and then strikes hard. He immediately raises his rod high and leans on it in order to get the fish away from the bank. This fish is way bigger than any he had hooked this morning, and this gets Jerry fired up. The fish runs short distances and repeatedly jumps and writhes in the air in an attempt to throw the hook, but it is in vain. Jerry has the fish in hand within minutes. He measures the big rainbow against his rod. It is twenty-four inches long and almost twelve inches in girth. Jerry releases the monster and sits on the bank, smiling. He keeps thinking how he had forgotten to tell Bobby to make sure his tippet size is beefed up. Jerry had tied his hopper to a ten-foot leader tapered to 1X tippet. Anything lighter, and he probably wouldn't have been able to land that fish.

Jerry knows that even though the fish were demanding during the trico spinner fall, these same fish lose their inhibitions when they decide on a meal the size of a hopper. During the event of a hatch or spinner fall, the fish are drawn to a certain type of insect with or without a particular type of movement. It is imperative to show these seemingly analytical trout something that is pretty close to the real thing. This means using line that is light enough so that the fish won't notice it and so that it will be supple enough in order to imitate the dead drift of the real insects. With the hopper, though, the fishes' demeanor is entirely different. This is not a meal that is sipped in or even expected. The grasshopper represents opportunity to a trout. It is a chance to ingest a huge amount of calories for one solid effort. Jerry knows that the hopper is a fly that the fish attack from some distance rather than consume by sitting under the surface film and sipping. A fish that decides to eat a hopper is not normally going to be dissuaded by tippet choice.

Jerry knows that the fish will see the hopper and attack it when they decide to eat big, and he hopes Bobby is aware of this, too.

Meanwhile, Bobby is downriver, going through exactly what Jerry had feared. It hasn't taken him long at all to hook a fish with his hopper pattern, but it also isn't long before he breaks this same fish off. Bobby is stuck on the fact that these fish are leader shy today. What he doesn't understand is that just because a fish is leader shy one moment doesn't mean it always will be.

Bobby breaks off the first fish of the afternoon on 5X tippet. The line parts the moment Bobby sets the hook. He stares at the water in dismay. The violence of the strike, compared to the delicate sipping he had seen in the morning, catches him off guard. He decides that his break-off was probably due to his overexcitement from the strike. He will cast again with a new fly, but this time he'll be sure to take it easy on the hook set.

Bobby ties on a new fly and casts slightly above where he had lost the first trout. There is no response. Bobby moves upstream a few yards and casts again. The fly is well under the grass, and, sure enough, this time there is a strike. He sees the fly vanish in a hole and hears the telling gulping sound. Bobby gently lifts the rod, and the fish is on. The big trout darts from the bank and violently shakes his head. The fly instantly comes loose, and the line goes slack. Bobby knows right away that he had not set the hook nearly hard enough in order to go into the fish's jaw. He again stares at the water, perplexed by the fix he is apparently in. He had thought that a heavy tippet would mean few or no strikes, while a light tippet wouldn't have the power needed to fish the big fly effectively.

Bobby decides to compromise and slightly beefs up his tippet to 4X. He moves upstream a bit and begins to fish the hopper fly again. The results are the same. In the next hour, Bobby breaks off three more large fish, loses two others on light hook sets, and manages to land just one fourteen-incher. He is about to hang it up for the day when he finally hears the distinctive jingle of Jerry's vest in the distance.

"Hey, how's it going there, Bobby?" Jerry says enthusiastically when he sees his friend.

Bobby responds, "Well, I've managed to decorate several fish with large flies and have pretty much been abused by the few I managed to hook up briefly."

Jerry was afraid of this and wishes he had told Bobby earlier to throw a really strong tippet. He doesn't have the heart to tell Bobby how well he had done upriver, so he stays off the subject. "I apologize, Bobby; I should have mentioned earlier about the trout's demeanor when it comes to hopper fishing. An angler can almost always use an extremely heavy tippet when fish have locked on the hopper. The trouts' feeding instinct tends to take over when hopper activity is high, and they lose inhibitions that may have been extremely strong only hours or even minutes earlier. This is apparent when heavy stonefly or cicada activity occurs as well."

Bobby checks out his leader set-up and compares it to Jerry's. "You must have your fly tied onto 1X tippet, Jerry," Bobby says. "You mean to say that these fish, which two hours ago wouldn't take a fly tied on 5X tippet, will now eat a fly tied to a 1X tippet?"

Jerry quickly answers, "They don't just take it; they take it with reckless abandon. A fish that wants to eat a hopper is not going to be denied. Something inside the trout's brain seems to snap, and it has to have the fly regardless of tippet size. Once you start experimenting with tippet diameters, you'll be shocked at what you can get away with. One other thing: As your fly-angling skills increase, especially line-on-the-water skills, you may find that you can catch fish on heavier tippets, rather than the lighter, more supple tippets that you used in the past in order to get the necessary drift to fool the fish. Don't hesitate to experiment, Bobby, and have faith in your abilities. The worst mistake a fly angler can make on heavily fished water is to get caught up in a routine. Be aware that the answers to the basic fishing questions are always changing out here on the water, and the anglers that have sound skills with knots, fly selection, fish location, presentation, and mending are going to be able to react more easily to new situations."

The two friends decide to fish a while longer so Bobby can see for himself that a fish's attitude toward leader shyness can differ from one moment to the next. He reties his leader and tapers the line to a 2X tippet. He continues fishing upstream while Jerry continues down. Half an hour later they meet back at the truck. Bobby had successfully landed three nice-size fish and had encountered no denials on his size 4 hopper pattern. He is amazed that the same fish can act so differently on the same day and is also amazed at how much more he feels he still has to learn when it comes to fly fishing. Jerry is always able to make the smallest observations work for him, he thinks, and keep other aspects from working against him.

Another day on Grassy Brook is complete, and both anglers agree that it was one of the best days they had ever spent fishing together. By the time Jerry pulls the truck into his drive-way it is well after dark. Before the anglers retire, they agree to look for Bobby's fish in the morning. The idea of fishing Fair-sized Creek keeps Bobby awake well into the night. Tomorrow just might be his day.

CHAPTER 12

USING A SEARCHING FLY

Bobby and Jerry are shocked when they arrive at the stream the next day. It is prime fishing season, the weather is beautiful, the wind is down, and the water levels and clarity are great, but there isn't a bug to be seen—in the air or on the water. Jerry shakes some streamside branches to see if a burst of caddis flies will fly out, but there is nothing in the vegetation either.

"I suppose we're fishing searching flies today, Bobby," Jerry says after a few minutes of observation.

Bobby asks, "Do you mean attractor patterns?"

Jerry rigs up his fly rod and replies, "You can use an attractor pattern, but what I mean by a searching fly is one that the trout may not eat, but it may be appealing enough for the trout to check it out and give itself away."

Bobby says, "Why don't we just use a dropper set-up if the fish aren't rising?"

"You can use a dropper set-up if you want, Bobby, but here's the thing. We are right in the middle of summer, and the conditions are brilliant, so I'm betting that the fish are going to be willing to rise to eat. For whatever reason, there just isn't any insect activity for the fish to dine on, so we're not seeing them, but I'm sure they're still going to be active. I've seen days like this before, and I think we can still catch all of our fish on the surface. When I use a searching fly, I am using a fly that I have a lot of confidence in. Attractors, flies in the stimulator family, and large terrestrials all work well. My personal favorite is a Royal Stimulator. It has the colors trout love and a convincing silhouette as well.

"With this fly, I should be able to get fish, even pressured fish, to rise up and look at it or flash it in the faster water. The fish here have seen enough angling pressure by now to know better than to eat the big searching fly most of the time, but on a day like this, when conditions couldn't be better, even the most stubborn fish should come and look at this fly.

"Experienced anglers can spot these sometimes subtle flashes on big flies without much trouble. Investing in good polarized sunglasses is a must for these situations. Once a fish is located, it becomes a simple matter of downsizing the fly to something more convincing and presenting it to the trout in an enticing way."

Bobby ties on a yellow size 8 Turk's Tarantula as Jerry finishes talking. "This has got to be my favorite fly. It is definitely the one I use most."

Jerry says, "Then that's it. The fly you have the most confidence in is the one that you should use. I'm going to walk up and start fishing in the hole above your big rainbow. Why don't you start here and work up to that run? If you're lucky, something may hatch or spin before you get up to where he is."

"That sounds good to me, Jerry, but I hope you're close by when I stick that big fish."

"I'm sure I'll hear it happening if it does," Jerry says. "Good luck!" he shouts over his shoulder as he disappears into the willow bushes.

Bobby wades into the stream just above the bridge where they had parked. He likes Jerry's point about the possibility of some insect activity starting before he gets up to the big rainbow's home stretch. He decides to take his time and fish very methodically upriver.

The sound of the water changes with each run that Bobby fishes. He hadn't noticed before what a major change there is as he fishes upstream from pool to pool. The day is as perfect as any he had previously seen in the Fairsized Creek valley. He catches a few fish on the Turk's Tarantula and sees a few flash it, just like Jerry said they would. When he sees the fish do this, he switches to a size 14 Irresistible Adams and manages to hook all but one of them.

He had fished halfway up to where the big trout had been before. He had caught several nice fish but had still seen zero bug activity. Bobby's had plenty of chances to catch the bruiser of a rainbow, and he has a feeling that he won't get many more before the fish finally vanishes. It looks like he may not get the opportunity to find the big trout today. He vows to remain patient and forces himself to continue methodically casting upstream. Maybe, just maybe, a hatch will materialize.

TERRANCE IS still in his favorite run. In this stretch of water, he had grown from one of many small fry to the magnificent and dominant specimen he is now. Through the course of the spring and summer Terrance had only been hooked three times, escaping each time. He is now about as big as he will ever get. He dwarfs the other fish around him by several pounds, and they stay well clear of him when he moves from spot to spot. He is not an old fish per se, just fully matured. Terrance dominates his underwater world.

Today there is little to eat in the river, but the currents of the stream are a comfortable temperature, and the spring flows had subsided enough so that Terrance can hang out in the currents below the riffles. He slowly, almost imperceptibly, combs the gravel for a morsel to eat. He keeps an eye out for small bait fish stuck in the current, and through his lateral line stays aware of any splash overhead that may signal trouble or even an easy meal. He drops to the back end of the riffles and feels and sees a big yellow mass drifting down toward him.

IT IS WELL after noon by the time Bobby fishes his way up to the monster trout's run. Jerry is nowhere in sight, and there are still no bugs. The surface shows no signs of fish, but Bobby stands, watches, and waits anyway. He had already caught some nice fish today, so he isn't in any rush to get his line in the water. Five minutes go by, and then five more. Bobby sees nothing come to the surface. Shadows are slowly beginning to darken the far bank, so Bobby decides it is better to fish now while he can still see the trout flashing at his fly in the sunlight. He wades slowly out, starting in the very back of the run.

Bobby makes a few casts to the flat water behind the mid-run riffles. Nothing takes his offering, and he sees nothing flash toward it. He takes a few steps upstream and casts again. How can Jerry be sure that the big 'bow is still living here? The odds of that happening are extraordinary. Bobby doesn't think he'll ever find out.

At about the same moment these thoughts are going through Bobby's mind, his yellow Tarantula bobs down the last few riffles above the flat water. He is just lifting the line to cast again when he thinks he sees a glimmer beneath his fly. That's all it is though, just a glimmer. It isn't the same pronounced flash he had seen earlier. This is more like the glint of sunlight seen coming off the window of a distant house as you drive a quiet country highway. You can't see the house in the distance, but you know something is out there.

It is enough for Bobby. He saw what he saw, and he isn't going to try to convince himself that he didn't see it. Bobby takes a few steps back and ties on a new pattern, a Green Drake Cripple. The real drake hadn't been on the water in months, but Bobby reckons that there have to be some bigger bugs this time of year. Most days of the summer there are smorgasbords of bugs, so the cripple effect is bound to imitate something. The fact of the matter is, Bobby is extremely confident in the cripple pattern design, and the drake is the biggest representation of it that he has. He ties the fly with a Duncan loop and takes the time to dress it properly.

Bobby looks up to where he had seen the glimmer. He doesn't know if what he had seen is his fish, but he is sure of where he had seen the glint, and he casts a few feet above it. The big cripple sinks halfway into the film and drifts downstream a few feet. It arrives where Bobby is sure he had seen the glint of light, and then, suddenly, there is a huge flash under the fly. The entire area of water beneath the fly seems to light up and turns pure silver. Bobby instantly knows that this is his fish. He has never seen anything so big and bright near his fly. The only problem is, the fish isn't taking the fly. Bobby's hands tremble. He looks upstream, stretching his neck, trying to get a glimpse of Jerry, but he can't see him. Bobby swings around and checks the log Jerry always sits on to see if he is there, but he's not. Bobby isn't sure what to do, and he desperately wants to ask his friend for help.

He accepts that he is on his own and begins to seriously ponder his situation. It only takes a few moments for Bobby to decide what course of action to take: none at all. He is still extremely confident in his fly choice. He begins to false cast the same fly to the same spot. The fly hits the water right where Bobby wants it, and he makes a small upstream mend to ensure no downstream drag on the fly. All at once, his hands stop trembling, and the fly drifts perfectly to the spot where the flash had happened only seconds earlier.

This time the fish is in no hurry. Bobby watches as a huge shape rises from the bottom. Almost effortlessly, a huge trout's head rises from the water. Bobby can see the mouth open and close around his fly. It is like watching a slow-motion jump shot in basketball. The outcome is often clear, but you still have to wait an eternity to see it. The fish finally disappears with the cripple fly, and Bobby raises the rod with a sure lift. The hook penetrates the fish's jaw, and water begins to fly.

Bobby is awed as the huge rainbow tail dances through the flat water below him. The big 'bow is acting like a sailfish, fighting in the air as much as in the water. The fish then makes a powerful upstream run into the fast water near the center of the pool. Bobby is concerned about wrapping the line on a rock, so he lifts the rod high over his head and pulls as hard as he dares.

The trout doesn't like the added pressure and responds by rushing downstream at him and cartwheeling twice out of the water, right under Bobby's rod tip. This almost sends Bobby into the water on his rear, but he is able to shuffle his feet and steady himself in the thigh-deep current. The mighty fish then bolts for the tail of the run again. He is heading for the rapids at the head of the next run downstream, and Bobby knows he will most likely lose him in the rough water. He turns the rod hard to the side and tries to coax the big 'bow back upriver. It's a standoff. Bobby pulls as hard as he dares, but the fish isn't budging. He can see the big fish sideways underwater thirty feet below him, still trying to get into the fast water of the next run downriver.

After three or four minutes of this, the fish finally moves again and slowly begins to swim back upriver. Only this time it swims slowly. As it swims past Bobby, the fish acts as if it isn't hooked at all. It swims right on by and begins to pull hard up into the middle of the current again. Bobby decides to let the fish sit there for a while this time. In this position, it will have to fight the current as well as the pull of the line. After a minute or two, Bobby begins to apply slow, even pressure, and after a few heart-pounding moments, he feels the fish begin to slowly rise to the surface.

Bobby feels that this reaction is his chance to head for the bank. He pulls the fish across the current with him as he goes, until eventually the weight of the fish drops it downstream of Bobby once more. He leans the rod toward the slower water near the bank he is now standing on, but the trout doesn't like it a bit

and heads directly across the current from Bobby. It jumps
halfway out of the water and then sits on the bottom in the current on the far side of the creek. Bobby decides that it's now or
never. He knows the hook will come out of the fish's mouth
soon, so he again pulls on the fish as hard as he dares. He had
heard Jerry talk about red lining his fly rod, and now he knows
what he meant by that. He takes the rod and the line to the edge
of its breaking strength, and the fish again begins to move.

The big rainbow reluctantly comes back across the current. It tries hard to gain the center of the river with short bursts several times, but Bobby has the fish worn down. With one last steady pull to the side, Bobby is able to put the fish on very shallow gravel in about six inches of water. He walks up to it and grins. The muscles on his face soon hurt as his grin widens. He kneels down and removes his fly from the biggest fish he has ever caught with a fly rod. He grabs a tape measure and places the tape down the length of the fish. This rainbow, which he had wanted so badly to catch, is a full twenty-five inches long.

Bobby lightly cradles the trout's belly and turns the fish into the current. With his other hand he holds the fish just above the tail, which he can't close his fingers around. He admires the fish's large spots and beautiful green back. The rainbow stripe down the side of the trout is laced with several shades of lavender and red. As Bobby turns the fish from side to side in the afternoon light, it almost looks like a hologram: Every angle looks like a different fish. Bobby watches the fish's gills work in the current, pumping and straining the precious oxygen from the liquid world. If only the fish could know what this means to him, Bobby thinks. The fish kicks to life in the cool, clean, reviving waters, and Bobby encourages him to swim off. The fish swims away with a burst of energy, but Bobby's grin stays perfectly intact.

The grin finally does fade when Bobby thinks about Jerry. In the end, he hadn't been there to see Bobby catch the big 'bow. After all, Jerry's guidance and advice had enabled Bobby to catch this fish. Now it would only be a story told by Bobby instead of a shared event. Without Jerry there to see it, it was anticlimactic.

Bobby is proud of himself, but this just isn't the way he had pictured it happening. Then he hears a voice:

"That was awesome!" Only it isn't a familiar voice. He looks back in the direction of Jerry's favorite log, and, sure enough, there is someone sitting there.

"Mister, you are the greatest fisherman I've ever seen!" says a boy who looks roughly to be ten years old. He had apparently been sitting on the log and seen the whole thing. How had Bobby not seen the boy when he looked back for Jerry? Bobby's smile returns.

Bobby stands up and says, "That was quite some fish, wasn't it, partner?"

The boy answers, "Mister, that is the biggest fish I've ever seen. Can you teach me to catch a fish like that?"

Bobby shakes his head. "Oh, I don't know. Where is your dad?"

The child quickly responds, "I just moved here with my mom. My name's Emmit. Can you teach me to fish like that?"

Bobby can't believe what is happening; after catching just one fish he is being asked to go from student to teacher. Who is this kid? The boy has long, greasy hair and wears cut-off shorts and an adult's dress shirt with the sleeves rolled up. The breast pocket is stuffed with fishing gadgets. He has an old, beat-up cane rod with him and a hat full of obviously home-tied flies. How can Bobby say no to this?

"Come over here, Emmit, and bring your stuff." The child's grin grows as big as Bobby's. The two new friends swap stories and fish the river together for the next half hour. Emmit catches a nice fish with a dropper fly. He had never seen this done until Bobby showed him, and Emmit can't wait to show his mom.

Not long after releasing a respectable fourteen-inch fish, the two new angling buddies see Jerry come ambling down the river. Bobby introduces them, and before he can say anything else, Emmit exclaims, "Mister, you should have seen it! My friend Bobby is the greatest fly angler to ever live. He was standing out there in the water, and I saw this fish eat his fly, and then . . ."

Emmit talks faster and faster, telling the story of Bobby and the monster trout as the three anglers head back downstream toward the bridge. Jerry and Bobby can't get a word in edgewise as Emmit tells the story without stopping to take a breath. As they arrive at the truck, Emmit asks the two more experienced anglers to meet him at the bridge early the next morning for round two. Bobby and Jerry agree, as long as it's okay with Emmit's mother. They give Emmit Jerry's phone number and say good-bye. He hops on his bike and rides off, eager to tell his mom about his new friends.

Jerry and Bobby smile as their new fishing buddy pedals away. Jerry congratulates Bobby on his fish with a firm pat on the shoulder, and Bobby thanks Jerry for all his help and friendship over the last year. They climb in the truck and head for Stuva's Grill. After all, there is a celebration in order.

TERRANCE HAD run into the angry insect again, only this time he hadn't been able to free himself until the large predator let him escape. He had fought hard and is exhausted, but he is able to regain enough strength to swim to the back eddy and sit on the bottom. He will stay put there and recuperate until darkness falls.

Just before all the light leaves the pool for the day, Terrance sees something move near a rock on the bottom. He swims forward a few feet, just in time to see a large stonefly nymph vanish under a good-size cobble. He sits near the rock and stares, waiting for Fairsized Creek to deliver his next meal.

GLOSSARY

back eddy. Places in rivers where the effect of the bank's contours makes the current turn and go back upstream in a circular motion. Lots of surface debris, foam, and insects collect in these areas. These are favorite homes of tricky trout.

CDC. Stands for the French words that mean "butt of the duck." CDC feathers come from the ass end of the duck. They have remarkable buoyancy, especially when treated with a dry-shake floatant. In recent years fly tyers have found many creative uses for these feathers.

Cuban cigar. A smoker's delight, held in very high regard by fly anglers around the world. It is also true that they really are better than every other cigar. An excellent way to show your fishing guides how much you appreciate them.

cripple fly. Flies that cannot escape from their nymphal shuck during an emergence. They are stuck in the water and become easy meals for hungry trout.

dead drift. The act of getting one's fly to float down a current lane with no pulling effect of the line and leader. The artificial should float exactly like the natural: not too fast or slow and not pulling across current lines.

dry fly. An artificial imitation of a winged insect (either a dun or a spinner) on the water.

dun. The "birth" of the winged insect. The dun is the freshly emerged bug that will leave the water but return as a spinner later.

emerger fly. An imitation of a nymph that is transitioning into a winged insect. This may take place anywhere or everywhere in the water column, depending on the type of insect. Fish key on specific stages of a bug's life, and during a hatch situation the emerger becomes very important.

false cast. The act of feeding line out while casting, or positioning the fly for the presentation. False casting also keeps dry flies dry.

floatant. A grease or powder that may be applied to a dry fly to keep it floating. Grease is most often used as a sealant, while the powders are used to dry a fly after it's been wet. Powders may also be used to float specific parts of flies for greater visibility.

leader. The section of line between the fly and the fly line. The leader is tapered from larger to smaller diameter.

mend. To manipulate the fly line on the water during a drift in order to get the fly to act a certain way depending on what the angler is trying to accomplish with his or her artificial imitation.

nymph fly. An artificial imitation of an aquatic insect; normally fished on a dead drift with a strike indicator or on a tight line swinging underwater.

presentation. The act of laying the line down on the water and presenting the fly to the fish or spot.

reach cast. A cast performed by reaching the rod across one's body or away from one's body, effectively turning the direction of the line. Reach casting is a way to mend the fly line before it ever hits the water.

riffle. The appearance of surface water as it runs over gravel and shallow spots. It is not quite white water but not flat water, either. Often pyramid shaped and sparkling.

spent wing. An aquatic insect that has died after spinning and whose wings have gone flat on the water.

spinner fall. Takes place when the insects return to the water. The insects mate; lay their eggs in, on, or above the water; and die shortly thereafter.

tailout. The back end of the run before the water pours into the next downstream rapid. A usually calmer section of water where fish go to eat on smaller, hard-to-see insects.

tippet. Spools of monofilament with even diameters; designated by an X, such as 5X or 6X tippet. Tippets are used to build leaders per specific angling situations.

trailing shuck. The nymphal shuck that is still attached to the back end of an aquatic insect as it attempts to wriggle free from it into a fully emerged dun. Cripple flies may never shed the trailing shuck, and it is not uncommon for fish to key in on this.

Zing Wing. A common synthetic tying material that is often used to bundle newspapers. It is a fantastic wing material to use when imitating a spent-winged insect.

Z-lon. A synthetic and fibrous, but supple, material. Z-lon has many uses in fly tying and is a great material with which to tie trailing shucks.